BAY'S END

EDWARD LORN

Bay's End

Also by Edward Lorn

Dastardly Bastard
Hope for the Wicked
Life after Dane
Cruelty
Fog Warning
Pennies for the Damned
Fairy Lights
The Sound of Broken Ribs
The Bedding of Boys
Everything is Horrible How
No Home for Boys

Collections

What the Dark Brings
Others & Oddities
Word

This book is dedicated to Chelle and Autumn, for allowing this, loving me unconditionally and, finally, for believing.

6

"Monsters are real, ghosts are real, too. They live inside us, and sometimes, they win."

—Stephen King

Interlude 1: A Place of Ghosts

I'm living with ghosts. My memories have grown legs and now run up and down these halls. The apparitions are only loops, broken records as it were, but they're aggravated and bored, two attributes you never want in a ghost. I've seen them in the kitchen, in the foyer, on the couch, and in the reflections on windows on a cloudy day. Nothing more than past events with faces and opinions. As Trent Reznor once said, "A fading, fucking reminder of who I used to be."

I don't want your sympathy. No, just the opposite. I would like for you to understand that it wasn't always like this. Memories last because you need to remember. Sure, there are plenty of reasons to ignore them—i.e., getting on with life, lessened emotional turmoil, being over it, just to name a few—but forgetting is akin to kicking a heroin addiction. You need this. Can't live without it. And therein lies the problem.

When you live in the past, you live with regret. Hindsight is always 20/20 and all that. You have time to question yourself about what you did, ponder the outcome of your actions. You ask yourself, day in and day out, if you couldn't have done that one thing better. Experience alters reality. You cannot progress if you don't screw up every now and then. In turn, you live, you learn. At least, that's what I've always been told.

The golden rule is: Do not listen. *If you don't listen to yourself, or the ghosts parading around pretending to be more than just ethereal reminders, you can live without regret. We are creatures of error, whether benign or malevolent, and our ghosts feed off our faults. Remember the lesson, not the failure. Move on, for Christ's sake.*

I just wish I could take my own advice. I suppose by writing this I will be labeled a hypocrite. Here I am, dwelling on past events, while I preach to you about the joys of forgetting. Still, I feel this tale needs to be told. It's not pretty. It's filled with some rather nasty shit that, I must confess, may turn a few heads, along with some stomachs. Nonetheless, they have to be brought up. If only for my own benefit. Call it cathartic. Call it therapy. Call it what you will. I tell you these things because I am trying to exorcise a few demons, and the fucking stair-master is broken.

So here it is, nothing more than abstract bullshit. My final story.

Chapter One: Eddy Treemont

I

July 1, 1992

People not from around here always think the name of my town is a typo. It's not. We don't have a bay. The nearest body of water is a hundred miles away. However, we did have a Francis Bay. He founded the town and died here. Some say it was the town that killed him. This place—this wonderful, horrible place—truly was Bay's end.

*

I met Eddy the weekend after his parents moved in across the street from us. He was a kid; I was a kid. It was summer in Bay's End, and we did what kids do. Like opposite-pole magnets, we were drawn to each other. It's that weird thing— you know what I'm talking about—how certain species of animals will go to the ends of the earth just to be with their own kind. Kids are like that. If there's another child nearby even close to his own age, that kid will seek him out, partner up with him and become lifelong friends. That's what they think, at least.

Eddy and I were no different. He was a little speck of a kid, almost a foot shorter than I was, but he swore that his mother promised he'd grow into himself. Whatever that meant. Eddy had a buck-toothed smile that went from ear to ear, and I found myself fascinated by his teeth. I would tell people—not him, of course—that Eddy could bite through inch-thick plate steel if he had to. He wore glasses, also, wire-rim things that made his eyes cross. My mother always told me they crossed because Eddy didn't really need glasses, but I couldn't understand why someone would wear something that made them look so utterly foolish if he didn't really need them.

Eddy was from Toledo, and even though I had no idea where that was, he said it was really nice, and he hadn't wanted to leave. He'd left some friends back there, and he missed them like *whores missed dick*—a saying he'd gotten from his father.

The first thing that drew me to him was the state of his jeans. I was a baseball player, and my jeans were always stained with green and utterly ridden with holes. My mother had fixed them up until the point I started ripping the fixes, too, then she finally threw in the towel and resorted to buying me new ones. Eddy's jeans looked just like mine. I hoped beyond a child's hope that the little guy played baseball, too. Needless to say, I was right. Eddy didn't just play baseball; he lived it.

The day was hot and dry. I was mowing the grass out in the front yard when the elderly Ford chugged up the street. The sound of the old diesel could be heard clearly over my mower's engine, and at first, I thought I'd broken the contraption. I let go of the idle, and the motor chugged once more before dying. The sound only got louder. I turned to look down Hibiscus Street to find the source of the rumbling. The Ford was rusted out and looked older than my grandfather. I surmised the thing was on its last legs, or wheels. At one point in time, ages ago, the paint had been a shade of sky blue, and in places, that color still snuck out for a peek. The little boy I would come to know as Eddy sat in the middle of the bench seat, his head barely showing over the dash, sandwiched between a pretty lady with corn-yellow hair and a burly old coot with a graying brown beard.

The aged Ford backfired as it pulled into the driveway across the street. Since the previous owner had sold the house, I automatically knew that the occupants of the car were the new tenants. When I realized that fact, my smile couldn't have gotten any bigger.

It had been almost a year since my buddy Aaron had moved to Wisconsin, and the Lance boys, Ryan and Jamie, never came out to play anymore since their mom died. They were a year younger than I was. The only reason I ever really hung out with them was because they lived on the same street. To say I was excited would be an understatement.

Eddy's mother got out of the busted truck first. She tucked her flowing blue skirt under her backside while she walked, and I thought that was quite odd. Eddy came sliding out next, all bouncy like one of those punch-me clowns, tilting this way and that, hopping like a bunny on crack. Mr. Treemont spilled out of the driver's side of the truck like a Jell-O blob being unhinged from a baking sheet. God, but that man had a presence. He looked to weigh a ton, and his belly very nearly reached his kneecaps. I remember thinking that his poor wife had better rethink her sleeping situation before she got crushed in her sleep if he ever happened to roll over on her.

Mr. Treemont was the first of the three to notice me. He nodded in my direction, and I nodded back, giggling inwardly as his second chin jiggled. He took a large box from the bed of the truck and balanced it on his gut. They walked to the front door, parents side by side and Eddy following. Mrs. Treemont unlocked the door to their new home. I will never forget how Eddy spun around on the porch just before going inside. Jumping up and down like a piston, he waved a limp hand at me and stuck up the middle finger on his other hand. I waved back, and he disappeared through the door.

I left the mower in the half-finished yard and bounded up the front steps of my home. Bursting through the front door and into the foyer, I ran past my father, who was sitting in the living room watching a Cubs game. We didn't live anywhere near Chicago and the Cubs always lost, so I had no idea why he favored them. Squealing and panting, I blew into the kitchen where my mom was fixing tuna for lunch.

"There's a... new kid... 'cross the street!" I placed my hands on my knees as I bent over to catch my breath. "Right... over there... new kid," I wheezed.

"Calm down, Trey." She ruffled my hair. "You knew someone was going to move in eventually."

"Mom, he's my age. Least he looks like he's my age. His dad's huge! His mom kinda looks like you. And their truck! Boy, does it look like a pile of—"

"Trey?" she stopped me before I screwed up and cussed in front of her. My father had a wayward tongue, and it was everything Mom could do to keep me from repeating every word that flowed from his mouth like verbal diarrhea.

"Fucking catch the goddamn ball, you queer bastard! Shit!" Dad yelled.

"Can I go over and say hello, Mom? Please, please, please, can I?"

"Is the yard done?" She smiled, knowing the answer already.

"But, Mom..."

"You've got to finish that yard, Trey. If you can manage to get it done, front and back—"

"Front *and* back?"

"—by tomorrow, then you can go over this weekend."

"This weekend? That's three days away!"

"Trey, listen to your mother!" Dad barked from the living room, "Assnuts catcher can't call a pitch to save his mother—"

"Daniel!" Mom never called Dad by his first name unless she was frustrated. "Please, it's just a game."

"Sorry, boobie." Dad had called Mom that for as long as I could remember. "Damn catcher, pft..." He lowered his voice, but I still heard him.

"Anyway," Mom said, "you get that yard done, and you can go meet him this weekend. You have to give them time to settle in, Trey. Trust me on this."

"Awww, all right." I lowered my head, trying to look pitiful.

"Buck up, Chuck. I'm sure you guys will hit it off, just not until this weekend." She laughed as she went back to her tuna sandwich preparations.

I kicked the carpet as I walked, making my disappointment known, or trying to, since Dad was so engulfed in yet another Cubs defeat. I could still hear him cussing Dawson, the right fielder, as I stepped out onto the porch and closed the door behind me.

Forlorn, I watched Mr. Treemont unload more boxes from the back of the truck. It took three hard tugs to get the old mower running again, but while I did that, I was privy to the arrival of an old Penske moving van. The thing was so big it completely blocked my view of the house. As the mower roared to life, I again zigzagged across the lawn, though I never really stopped watching. Two big black guys unloaded the back of the moving truck with Mr. Treemont's help. It went on that way for a good hour before I finally had to stop and add gas to the lawnmower.

I didn't like the fact that I was going to miss everything while I trudged around the side of the house to mow the backyard. It sucked, to tell you the truth, and I wished I had mowed the back of the house first. Cursing my situation, I started the engine, which took five tugs that time, and set to work as the sun went down behind the world.

II

The first thing Eddy Treemont said to me on Saturday afternoon was also the last thing he said to me the day he died.

"Whataya lookin' at, shithead?"

Eddy stood in the door of his new home with a big grin on his face that would rival the Joker's in any Batman comic. His shirt said everything I needed to know about him, and I coveted it because it was so damn grown up: "If it has tits or tires, it'll give you trouble..." I loved it!

"Hey, I'm Trey Franklin." I smiled. "I was wondering, um, if you wanted to, you know, hang

23

out?" My words came off meek and unlike me, but the way he'd answered the door caught me off guard.

"Mom!" Eddy yelled back into the house with a turn of his slender neck.

"Yeah?" a light female voice answered.

"Going out with the neighbor kid! His name's Trey, and he lives across the street. Looks like a cool cat!" I liked the kid already.

"Be back by dark, jerk!"

"Thanks, bitch!"

My mouth dropped open, and I fully expected to see that yellow-headed woman charge down the hallway to snatch him up by his collar, but she never did. Eddy just closed the door and skipped down the steps leaving me on the porch with my mouth catching flies.

"You coming?" Eddy called as he ran into the street.

I jogged down the steps and ran to his side.

"So, what's there to do around here?" Eddy asked, shoving his hands deep into his tattered jeans. They were different jeans than the ones he had worn the day I first saw him, but in just as bad shape. There was a hole under his right back pocket, and I saw he had the same problem with streaking as my father and I had. What was it about boys and not wiping properly?

"There's the ballpark over behind the high school; Rifle Park is kinda cool. I like to go out to the Westerns and hang out in the old buildings."

"The Westerns?" Eddy kicked a random rock out of his way. We were walking toward the end of Hibiscus, with him leading as though he knew where we were going.

"It's what the old folks call the western edge of Bay's End. It's full of old derelict logging buildings they closed back when the government and environment people moved in. Really just old hollowed-out structures, is all." I kicked my own rock.

"Sounds creepy."

"Yeah. I like it."

"Where's the ballfield again?"

"Behind the high school."

"I think we passed it on the way into town. Didn't look like much." Eddy's foot found another rock and sent it ricocheting off the curb. It was becoming a competition of sorts.

"Your mom lets you call her a bitch?" I finally asked after a moment of silence.

"She called me a jerk." He shrugged.

"Yeah, but... she's your mom, dude." The rock that struck the curb bounded back toward me, and I sent it flying into a drainage culvert.

"So?" Eddy looked over at me and grinned. I would get used to that smile over the next couple weeks, but at that time, it still seemed pretty odd. "Which way?"

"Huh?" I asked, preoccupied with the fact that he saw nothing wrong with cussing his mother, and that she didn't seem to mind, either.

"I don't know which way to turn, man. Remember, I'm new here."

"Oh, that. You wanna see the Westerns or the ballfield?" I asked.

"Neither. Just take me somewhere cool."

"Right on." I smiled, and Eddy gave me another glimpse of his buck-toothed grin.

Bearing right onto Lime Street, which crossed Hibiscus, we started toward Rifle Park. I assumed it was a cool enough place. I could show him the pile of timber that would become the annual bonfire toward the end of summer. I thought he would get a kick out of that. I really didn't have anything to go off of, no idea what he thought was cool or otherwise. Part of the fun was getting to know each other.

At the end of Lime, while we ruminated on the Dodgers' shitty season and how in the world the Cubs were ever going to win one with *The Wild Thing* pitching lopsided like he did, we turned right onto Fir. Every road in the town, aside from Main, was named after some kind of plant, tree, or obtuse vegetation, and Eddy mentioned it as we came up on Sequoia Avenue.

"What the fuck is that?" Eddy asked, wide-eyed and holding a hand to his chest.

"That, dude, is Romo." I laughed, but it was forced. Romo scared the stains out of my pants worse than any monster I'd ever seen in any movie, and the last thing the thought of him made me want to do was laugh. But I couldn't let Eddy think I was a big baby, either.

"Row-mo?"

"Yeah, Romo. Some kinda half-breed wolf all jumbled up with several other dogs. My mom says it's just pissed because of an identity crisis or something like that. It doesn't help that the neighborhood kids throw rocks at him on their way to school."

"That's jacked up, man." Eddy whistled, which I thought was quite a feat given his large front teeth.

"Sanders owns the thing. Normally, he'd be out with us, but he's all grounded and shit from throwing rocks through windows out at the Westerns. Officer Mack caught him the first week of summer, and I ain't seen him since."

"Fucked up."

"Yep." I pointed toward Sanders's yard as we approached. "See him. Big bastard, isn't he?"

"Shit, man, he's huge!" Eddy said.

Romo sat where he normally did, in the runner alongside the house. Sanders's dad had built the thing after Romo had almost ripped Tony Marchesini's ass off the previous winter.

We had been coming home from school the final week before Christmas vacation when Tony Marchesini tossed a baseball-sized rock at the mutt. Romo grunted as the stone flew past his head, not even flinching. Instead of retreating like a normal dog, Romo leaped over the four-foot fence as if it were only an inch tall. Tony turned tail and ran, but he wasn't fast enough. That beast of a canine latched onto Marchesini's back thigh as if it were a honey baked ham. Tony lay in the middle of the street, Romo wrestling the ass off him, while Candice Waters and I ran onto Sanders's porch to get help. Mr. Sanderson had to use mace on the hell hound before it would let loose of Tony. It was the craziest nonsense I'd seen in my life.

Romo growled, barked, and salivated something fierce as Eddy and I passed its yard. I could almost read Romo's thoughts. "Go on, throw a rock. Throw a rock. I *fucking* dare you!" I had never teased the dog and didn't intend to, but Romo didn't know that. Dog's memories were like baseball cards—just a picture and some important need-to-know facts. My picture was in Romo's head, right next to all the thrown rocks since I *had* been in the vicinity pretty often when other kids had thrown them. He didn't care that I hadn't actually partaken in the torment; he only cared that I had been present.

"You think he eats nails and shits barbed wire?" Eddy slugged me in the shoulder, laughing.

"Likely." I chuckled.

"Dad says that a lot about the wrestlers on TV. 'They must eat nails and shit out barbwire, Myrtle,' he always tells Mom. 'Boy like mine gonna do the same thing, huh, Champ?' That's me; I'm Champ, least to Dad I am." Eddy started back along Sequoia, again as if he knew where he was going. It was uncanny, watching him walk with such confidence, even though he couldn't

29

have known the way. That was Eddy, for the most part. Head first, questions postponed for a later date.

"Your dad a pretty all right guy?" I felt the need to ask.

"He's fucking *awesome*. Drinks like a goon, but he's a cool drunk. Funnier than hell if you ask me and Mom. Mom don't drink much, but she says Dad lays the pipe better when he's sloshed, so she doesn't mind."

"Your dad's a plumber?"

Eddy laughed. "Nah, man. It means fucking. You know, layin' pipe?"

"Huh?"

"Never mind." He shook his head. "How old are you, man?"

"Almost thirteen. Why?"

"You're 'bout old as I am, and you don't know what layin' pipe means?" Still laughing, Eddy kicked another rock, first one for that street.

I set foot to one of my own. "Dad's got *Playboy*s, but they don't show that kinda stuff. Cinemax does, though. You know, late night on the weekends. They 'lay pipe' in those movies."

"Don't say that." Eddy cackled uncontrollably, doubling over from the effort, his voice cracking.

"What?" I asked.

"Don't ever say 'laying pipe' again. Just don't. Oh... I can't... breathe."

We laughed for a good block and a half, not really saying anything else, not really needing to. I remember that sound even now. It was childhood; it was innocence. We did what kids did. We laughed, we played, we shot the shit, and we lived.

It was perfect, if only for a moment.

III

I woke up to soft tinkling on my bedroom window. Sitting up in bed, I wiped the gunk from the corners of my eyes. I picked up my alarm clock to check the time: two o'clock in the morning! Feeling an eerie sense of impending doom, I decided to stay in bed, just go back to sleep. I had seen *Salem's Lot. Only bad things tapped on your window while you slept.*

"Trey! Yo, Trey!"

"Huh?" In the glow of the moonlight coming in through my shades, I saw the mirror image of myself looking like a pile of pale flesh in striped pajamas. For a moment, I thought my reflection had awakened me. I was about to ask myself what I wanted, when I heard a voice that definitely wasn't mine, and certainly did not belong to my pallid doppelganger residing in the looking glass.

"Open your fucking window, man," Eddy said.

"I'm coming," I whispered, doubting he had actually heard me.

I slid on my slippers and made my way to the window. Raising my blinds slowly, trying not to wake the parents, I clicked the cord into place to keep them open. Eddy stood just beyond the glass, his head snapping back and forth, ever vigilant. I wasn't really sure he was afraid of the dark so much as he was of getting caught. He didn't look as though he had fangs, and his face wasn't bloodless in the dim light, so I figured opening the window wouldn't hurt. I unlatched the clasp on the sill and slid up the window.

"What do you want, dude? It's like, you know, the middle of the night and shit," I asked, yawning.

"You wanna go out to the Westings?"

"It's the *Westerns*, and no. It's gonna be daylight soon," I said, fighting for a reason that wouldn't make me sound like too much of a coward.

"Stop making excuses, shithead." Obviously, I hadn't succeeded.

"But, dude, I might get caught."

"You won't get caught. No one sleeps lighter than my mother, and I got out just fine. And *your* window doesn't squeak."

I looked back toward my closed bedroom door half-expecting, half-hoping, Mom or Dad would come in and save me from screwing up. I turned back and nodded at Eddy. Leaving the window open, I went to my bed and arranged the pillows under the covers, making it look as if I were curled up in there somewhere. I pulled open my dresser drawer ever so slowly. It creaked once, but didn't give me away.

"Are those footie pajamas?" Eddy snickered.

"At least I change my clothes, dude," I said, pointing out the fact that he still wore his offensive T-shirt from earlier in the day.

"Yeah, well, fuck off with your onesie, dildo breath."

"You gonna watch me change, fag?"

"Don't you wish I sucked cock?" He made a fist and pumped it in front of his open mouth, his tongue poking his cheek in and out. He turned around after a few seconds, though.

"Smile like a doughnut and nod yes or no, bitch." I pulled a pair of ratty jeans from the second drawer of my dresser and a T-shirt from the first. After throwing them on, along with my socks from the previous day, I grabbed my Nikes out of the closet and slid into them. Ready to go, I struggled with how to get out of my window.

The drop wasn't more than two feet, but it was higher than my crotch. Easing one leg out of the frame, I rested my butt on the sill and slid sideways, hoping my foot would touch pay dirt before I fell out into the unseen expanse of yard below, breaking something important in the process. Finally, just before I lost my balance, my shoe touched the grass, and I was able to gain my footing before sliding out my other leg. I slid the window mostly closed, leaving it open enough for me to slide my fingers in when we returned.

When I turned around to face Eddy, he grinned, a mischievous buck-toothed expression turned sinister by the light of the moon overhead.

"You ready?" Eddy asked, sounding wide-awake and bubbly.

"You sure you wanna do this, dude?"

"Kinda late for that question, ain't it?" He slugged me in the shoulder. "Come on, shithead, we got a lot of ground to cover."

"How do you know?"

Eddy started around the side of the house. "I used the maps of the town Dad picked up from the library when he first found our house. From what the legend says—"

"Wait. You can read?"

"Fuck you. Anyway, I used the legend... you know, measuring with my thumb and shit... and from what I gather, it's about two miles away, right?"

"Damn. You got that close using your thumb?"

"Yep, around three inches. I s'pose you coulda used your dick."

"What's with your fascination with cock tonight? Something I should know?"

We walked out into the sodium vapor street lights of the road. Eddy had an eerie glow about him under those jaundice rays. His grin looked malevolent, and a shiver ran up my spine.

"Dad asked me where we went today," Eddy said as we hit Lime for the second time in twenty-four hours.

"Yeah? What'd you tell him?"

"Told him about Romo."

"You getting at something with this?"

"He said he knows that Sanders kid's father. The guy hired him out at the school," Eddy said.

"Your dad's a teacher?" I asked, incredulously. The man sure didn't look the part. Aside from a cooking course, I really didn't see him teaching anyone's child anything important.

"Nah, that fat fuck? No way. Kids would give him so much shit. Nope, he's the new janitor."

I erupted in guffaws with that bit. "And kids won't make fun of him for that?"

"Fuck you, asshole. You know what I mean. Besides, he's an overnighter. Graveyard shift."

"Well, that's a little better, I guess," I said as I tried to stifle my laughter. After leaving Fir, we came up to Sequoia, and I was surprised when Romo didn't go nuts at our presence.

"What I was getting at is, my old man knows Sul... Sole... Sun..."

"Sulan?"

"Yeah, that's it. He knows Sulan Sanderson, the vice principal, I guess he is, and Sulan got my pops a job. Small world, huh?"

"Shit, yeah it is. Sulan isn't exactly, uh, friendly, Eddy. He rules Sanders with an iron fist most of the time. When Sanders isn't on restriction, he's busy with chores and studying."

"The guys a chink, right?" Eddy just said it as though it was all right, or something, as if that's just what you called Asian people.

I ignored it, but locked it up in my memory banks. Maybe Eddy meeting Sanders wasn't such a good idea. "He's Asian, yes. His wife's black, though."

"So, Sanders is a mutt just like his dog?" Eddy giggled. "Fucking priceless."

"He's my friend, dude." I tried to sound stern, but when I was around Eddy, everything seemed to come out too soft, as if I were holding something back, covering what I really wanted to say with weak rhetoric, placating him.

"Aw, nothing wrong with that, I don't suppose. This town's so small, you gotta make friends where you can."

"Funny thing is, I've never heard Romo this quiet." I squinted to look in the runner.

"Dad says that Sulan keeps him inside at night because some neighbors got to complaining and stuff."

"Oh." I nodded. "Makes sense."

"That's how I knew it would be cool to come this way." Eddy grinned, his bucks glinting in the moonlight.

"Why'd you wanna go to the Westerns tonight? Or this morning. Or shit, whatever it is."

"Seemed as good a time as any. I don't sleep right when Dad's giving Mom the hammer, if you know what I mean." Eddy pumped his fist as though cocking a shotgun.

"You mean layin' pipe."

"Quit that shit," Eddy said, having to stop as his giggles took him over. "You don't say it right, man!"

"Shut the fuck up out there!" a voice called from a window across the street.

"Oh, shit," Eddy hollered. He shot me a grin before he took off running. I followed, not because I was scared, but because it was fun. Nothing more than just good, old-fashioned, stupid fun.

IV

We left Sequoia and blew across Main Street. Running full tilt, we flew into Rifle Park and the safety of the tree line. A few feet into it, we found the stone pathway leading to the bonfire area. Since that wasn't where we were heading, we took off in the opposite direction. Cutting through to High Stone Pathway, named after the wall of granite that ran alongside it, we finally stopped to rest.

We bounced up and down in the darkness as we fought to catch our breath. Our laughing made it a little more difficult. I'd never felt like that, and I had Eddy to thank. Just one day, one single day, around that kid, and I was already sneaking out of the house and causing a ruckus in the neighborhood. If we got caught, Eddy would be considered a bad influence—I was sure of that little fact—and I couldn't lose him as a friend.

Funny how close you can get to someone after less than a day of knowing each other.

Eddy and I walked in silence from there on. Every now and again, he would look over at me and smile, and I would return the sentiment. It was that comfortable quiet that you could only share with family and close friends. It was really cool, or at least *I* thought so.

High Stone Pathway ended where Juniper Boulevard began. Juniper ran the course around the west edge of town and dead-ended directly into the Westerns. Moving along at a brisk clip, Eddy and I made it to the Westerns in a little less than an hour. We came upon the raggedy gates of the derelict monoliths, stopping only briefly to take in the decaying architecture.

The South Building, so called because those words were etched along the front of the place in one-story-tall white letters, was the largest of the buildings. The red paint had long ago dried and peeled, and you could only see tiny specks here and there that gave away its previous color. The rotted wood was cracked in places, giving the outside a fang-filled-mouth appearance. Even in the dark, I could tell Eddy felt the same way I did when I first saw the place—awestruck and extremely uneasy.

The Green House was cattycorner to the South Building. Dad said they'd made the roof out of green plastic because it saved on electricity. When I asked him why they hadn't just used clear plastic, he just shrugged and left my room. Dad was like that sometimes. The Green House was my favorite of the three structures, with its white paint-covered cinderblock walls. My least favorite was the last building located at the northern end of the property.

The Dark Room loomed in the distance, a cylindrical leviathan of brick and metal. The rounded structure looked like a grain silo, but I had no idea what use a logging company would have had for it. The building just scared the shit out of me, day or night, even though that night, it was especially disconcerting. The thing I always found the most unsettling about it was the lack of windows. I can only assume, even now, that was how it had gotten its name. Because once inside, you were covered in complete and unceasing darkness.

"You all right?" Eddy broke the silence, making me jump.

"Not anymore." I held my thumping heart in my chest. "Jesus, scary much?"

"Whatever." He grinned. "So these are the Westerns, huh? Fucking cool, dude." Eddy stared at those skeletal structures with a child's love of curious things, so different, I was sure, from the fear in my own eyes. He seemed hypnotized, drawn in. Eddy's teeth shined with saliva, and for a moment, I imagined him as a rabid beast eying its prey.

"Glad we came?" he asked.

"Sure," I lied.

"Come on." He moved toward the gate, and my heart sank.

"What? I'm not going in there at night. Are you out of it?" I shook my head and took several steps back.

"What did you think I wanted to come out here for? Just to fucking look? Get real, man. This shit is awesome."

"Yeah, and it's just as awesome in the daylight," I said. "Trust me on this."

"Man, come on. What's it going to hurt?" Eddy was almost to the point of begging, his voice shrill and whiny.

44

"Well..." I sighed, not really believing what I was about to say. "All right. Just for a minute, dude. For real."

"Yes!"

We scaled the chain-link as only boys our age could. Something was lost to adult males of our species. I'd watched several episodes of *Cops* in my time—with and without my parents' approval—and I'd seen all those officers struggling to traverse fences just like the ones we faced with ease. Whether it be fat, skinny, or otherwise, none of them had the flawless skill we kids seemed to carry, especially boys. Maybe it was a center of gravity thing, or a too-old thing, but whatever it was, at that moment, I was glad I was a kid.

Making quick work of the fence, we crashed down on the other side like cats—feet first. Eddy flashed me his buck-toothed grin, and I smiled back nervously. I could feel the presence of those three hulking buildings, seemingly shifting in the moonlight like breathing entities.

Eddy must've seen the terror in my eyes because he said, "Damn, man, you got issues with this place or what?"

"Not in the daylight," I responded.

"What's the difference? My old man always says, 'There's nothing there in the dark that ain't there in the light,' and I'm prone to believe him."

"He also says wrestlers shit nails and eat barbwire."

"It's the other way around. Well, kinda... man, you fucked that all up." Eddy shook his head. "Stop screwing up my father's words of wisdom, all right?"

"Deal." I laughed. "But only if we can go soon."

"Would you quit with that shit, man? It's getting to sound more and more like you got a wet slit between your legs."

"Would you please stop worrying about what's happening under my zipper, dude?"

"More like what's not happening there."

The gravel of the forgotten parking lot crunched under our shoes as we progressed. The full moon lit our way as we made it to the South Building first. I became increasingly concerned that he actually meant to go inside one of those places in the dark. For some odd reason, Mr. Treemont's voice played through my head, even though I hadn't heard the man speak: "There's nothing there in the dark that ain't there in the light."

Having found no entrance to South Building, we moved along the outer wall until we came to the Green House. Then, my nerves got the best of me. I knew the door on the easternmost side had been removed from its hinges, giving anyone who dared full access to the inside. That fact about drove me crazy. I knew in my heart of hearts that if Eddy found out, we'd be there exploring until dawn. Or he would, because I sure wasn't dancing with the devil by the pale moonlight.

Luckily, he skirted the Green House completely. But another problem arose where one had been solved.

Eddy was headed straight for the Dark Room.

"Dude," I whispered. I wasn't sure who I was trying to hide my voice from, but figured there must be *something* hiding in the shadows just waiting to pounce should I raise my voice.

"Yeah?"

"It's going to be sun up in just, like, you know... soon." I sounded like an idiot, but I didn't really care. I would have sold my right testicle at auction and pawned my left one to keep from going in that godforsaken place.

Eddy seemed to hear it in my voice. "Grow a pair, Trey. Shit, man."

I ignored him, as I would learn to do quite often in the following weeks. Eddy didn't seem to mean any harm; he just liked fucking with me. I resorted to just laughing at him when he made his smartass comments. What else was there to do? He was quickly becoming the best friend I'd ever had. I couldn't help but think of what Sanders would think of him, as Sanderson had previously been my best bud.

When I stood beside the Dark Room, it seemed forever tall, giving the expectation that somewhere up there, God kneeled chin to fist, like Rodin's *Thinker*. The place smelled of rotted wood and damp stone, not a pleasant mixture to the senses. Eddy thought it far too cool how wet the brick of the outer structure felt as he ran a hand across it, grinning like the Mad Hatter. When his hand came back slick with the stuff, he wiped it down the front of my shirt, and I squealed like a little girl.

"What the fuck you do that for?" I bellowed as I tried to slap the nasty filth from my chest.

"It's all gooey, Trey." He giggled. "Like Nickelodeon slime, right?"

"It's always like that, you dirty bastard! This shirt is all jacked up now."

"Calm down. Just throw it in the laundry before your mom gets up this morning. She won't know where and when you got it dirty. Trust me."

"Fuck!" I couldn't stop repeating the word. I'd never cussed like that before Eddy, and never after him. It just seemed to come naturally when I was around him.

I was stolen from the moment as my heart ceased to beat in my chest. Long shadows formed as blinding white light crawled up the length of the Dark Room's outer wall. I didn't know what I was seeing, but long black demons seemed to be coming toward me from the end of a bright tunnel. I was all set to run when I heard the bleat of a horn at our backs.

Whoop! Whoop!

"Sonuvabitch," Eddy said, sounding thoroughly defeated.

The spotlight faded, and the night went red and blue, the lights coalescing over and through each other, making purple on the stone wall of the Dark Room.

"Come outta there, boys. Fun's over!"

Chapter Two: Mack Larson

I

Lieutenant Mack Larson was a presence all by himself. The man stood over six feet tall and rose above most of us kids like a menacing behemoth. His breath always smelled like cherry lozenges, and his tongue was always red when it flicked out to lick his forever-chapped lips. He'd gotten the scar that ran down his right cheek in Vietnam when Charlie snuck up behind him and tried to slit his throat. Mack had bobbed and weaved just in time so the knife had missed his jugular, but opened his face like a Christmas gift.

Mack was the middle child in a family of five. His older brother, Harrison, was a Bay's End firefighter and was cherished throughout town. His younger sister, May Larson, was a math teacher at Bachman High and had been for over thirteen years. His parents had been teachers also, before they retired in the early eighties.

Yes, I knew every bit of this. Why? Because, it was common knowledge around The End. Mostly because Officer Mack ran the D.A.R.E. program at our school and loved telling us all about his illustrious family's roots. But just because Officer Mack was a well-loved member of the community and part of a famous group of teachers and public servants, that didn't mean he lacked a bad side. When he'd caught Sanders chucking rocks through the windows of South Building, Officer Mack had taken him home and had stayed to witness the pummeling Sulan Sanderson had dealt.

"He just stood there smiling," Sanders had whispered to me over the phone. He snuck the cordless into his room just to give me the news. The thought of Officer Mack just standing there while Sulan wailed on Sanders, that creepy scar stretching across his face as he smiled, made me about wet myself.

"Smiling?" I asked.

"Heck, yeah. Like the freaking Grinch," Sanders hissed into the receiver. The sound made my ear itch.

Our call was cut short by the fuming broken English of Sulan Sanderson. "What you doing?" *Smack.* "You no talk." *Whack.* "You don't get phone." *Thump.* "No privileges for you." *Crash.* The line went dead.

Even though I knew he wasn't there, I could see Officer Mack standing in Sanders's bedroom door with his hands upon his hips. Smiling. I shuddered as I hung up the phone.

In the dark of my room, I had said a silent prayer for a fallen comrade.

II

The night seemed colder as Eddy and I leaned up against the front of the police cruiser. Officer Mack stared at us from under the bill of his patrolman's cap while he scratched at his scarred cheek, working on the thing as if it would just *Poof!* disappear, if only he were diligent enough. His eyes were hollow, like tiny black dots on round, white canvasses, and they surveyed us with a calm calculation.

"Now." Mack cleared his throat, making the scent of cherries and menthol permeate the night air. "I don't know you." He pointed at Eddy. "But you're the Franklin's kid, ain't'cha?" he asked me.

"Yes, sir," I replied meekly.

"'Scuse me, boy?" He put a hand to his ear as if it would help him hear me better.

"Yes, Officer Mack," I said, louder that time, like a private to a drill instructor.

"That's better. Speak clearly when you talk to me. Hearing ain't so good no more, Franklin." Mack spit some red and brown gunk onto the road. The gooey substance congealed at my feet. I felt sick to my stomach already, and the crud he'd brought up from his lungs wasn't helping the matter. "Who's you, son?"

"Edwin Treemont," Eddy said, his voice coming out of him like a volcano erupting. He obviously didn't want to repeat himself, so he made sure Mack heard him the first time.

Mack glared at him. "New t' town?"

"Moved in 'cross the street from me three days—"

"Shuddit! I was talking to new blood o'er 'ere, Franklin." Mack's jarring tone shut me right up. Turning back to Eddy, he asked, "You moved into the old Jamison house?"

"I guess so." Eddy shrugged.

Mack apparently didn't like Eddy's flippant gesture, and I could do nothing but stand there and watch as he strode the three feet to get nose to nose with my new friend.

"'Scuse me, kid?"

"You heard me, dipshit."

I about crapped my pants. I couldn't believe what I'd heard, and neither could Mack, from the look on his face. I let out a quick blurt of laughter—whether nerves or humor-induced, I still don't know—and I instantly regretted it.

Mack flipped me around and shoved me belly first onto the hood of the car, all with a single hand. Eddy was whipped and slammed down beside me. Mack kicked our legs apart, growling, "Spread 'em."

"Officer Mack, Eddy didn't mean—"

"Shuddup, son. Just you be quiet. You boys got anything on you?"

"N-no, sir," I whimpered as the officer dug through my pockets like a pedophile looking for a thrill.

"You can't do this," Eddy said with not an ounce of fear in his voice.

I envied him that. With that one sentence, I felt he could watch the end of the world without so much as a blink. I longed to have that much courage, but I wasn't growing it that morning.

"I can do whatever the hell I please," Mack said, and I could almost see the smile stitch its way across that disfigured face. "See, 'ere, you boys are trespassing, an' I can't have that. So 'ere I come, upholding the law and everything, and you wanna question my right to post you up on the hood of my car to give you a proper inspection? I will be damned, son. I just will be damned all to H-E-double-fucking-hockey-sticks. Pardon my French, o'course."

"Just take us home, shit heel." Eddy bucked and sucked wind, hard, as he was repeatedly slammed into the hood.

Mack laughed. "You got a mouth on you, son. Don't'cha now?"

"He doesn't know you, Officer—"

"Damn straight he doesn't know me, or my family. Little shit—pardon my French—comes into this town like he knows e'erything 'bout e'erything," Mack said in a singsong lilt. "Well, you don't know bullcrap, son."

Eddy's body flopped again as Officer Mack dealt out his punishment. I felt helpless, hopeless, and scared. I could do nothing but lean there, bent over like some prison bitch while Mack tormented my new friend. I'd heard the stories about Mack, but I'd never seen it with my own eyes. I became a believer.

"Get off... me... you big... fuck," Eddy wheezed, his breath misting the hood of the cruiser.

Eddy reared back, pulled up by his hair, and Mack drove his forehead into the car hood. Eddy made a small noise, smaller than I thought possible, and his eyes rolled back in his head before they fluttered back to center.

"Put a leash on that yap 'fore I stifle it myself, son." Mack leaned into Eddy's back. "Now, where was I? Oh yeah, what the hell am I going to do with you?"

"Please, just take us home, Officer Mack," I begged. I was crying, and it didn't seem at all controllable as snot bubbles burst from my nose, wetting the cruiser's hood.

"Take you home and do what?" Mack asked.

I was shocked by the question, but it didn't hinder my quick response. "Tell our folks!" I blurted, too loud for what I'd intended. "Please, just take us home. I won't... won't tell anybody."

"Won't tell anybody what? What you did? Or what I'm doing?"

"Either," I whined. "Either, or. Please."

"Well, shit." He chuckled as though he'd heard the funniest thing in the world. "Since you put it that way."

Mack let up, and Eddy slid down the hood of the cruiser into a crumpled mess on the asphalt. Not caring at the moment what the repercussion of my actions would be, I dropped to Eddy's side and started shaking him. I didn't know what else to do, but I just couldn't let him be alone down there on the ground like that.

Eddy groaned and opened his eyes. "Hey, Trey. Whataya say?" His eyeballs swam in his head as he tried to focus on me. He looked pitiful, but somewhere in the back of my mind, I heard, "He deserved it. Should have kept his mouth shut." The voice belonged to Officer Mack, but the crooked cop hadn't said a word.

"Help 'im up," Mack said as he adjusted his belt.

For a split second, I thought he was going for his gun. Given the current events, I wouldn't have been surprised if he'd put two in both of our heads.

"Time to ride, boys." Officer Mack grinned sickly in the headlights before spitting another wad of crimson-colored gunk onto the ground.

III

Chief Harold "Hap" Carringer once said of Lieutenant Mack Larson, "It has been an honor and privilege to have known and worked with this man. He is, and always will be, a pillar of our community."

Hap Carringer had been chief of police in our little rural city since the late sixties, and everyone had made sure to send him off properly. The retirement party had the entire Bay's End township in attendance. There was music, food, and an open bar for the adults while the kids sipped fruit punch from plastic cups. Even after a doting from the soon-to-be-replaced chief, Mack Larson stood stoically, never cracking a smile. People danced in City Hall's Event Center, while Mack Larson sat up on the stage, ever watching.

I remember seeing him there, thinking that the guy must be lonely, what with the way he presided over the festivities. But now, I know better.

Mack Larson hadn't been watching. He'd been waiting.

As the day's events wore on, and night dropped like a ton of bricks, the liquor was having its effect. Jud Finke started the trouble first when he backed into Martin Goodwill's backside and his hand accidentally touched the other guy's butt. Both men had been drinking heavily the entire night, and I could tell by the way they dragged their sober wives across the dance floor that something was about to happen. Whether it would be humorous or tragic, I didn't know.

There were roars of "Faggot!" and "Asshole!" as the fight broke out. It wasn't like in the movies, not in the least. Not one clean punch was thrown as the two inebriated individuals tussled in the center of the dance floor. They writhed like two snakes mating, dropping in and out of each other's grasp. They tried failed-and-forgotten high school wrestling moves to bursts of laughter from the drunken audience. Jud threw a punch that actually landed on Marion's shoulder, and then he reeled back, waving his hand in the air as if it were on fire.

Mack Larson came out of thin air. There wasn't any warning, no call of "Break it up," just the sudden arrival of a very tall, mission-oriented man in a police uniform. He erupted from the crowd all chest and biceps and scarred face, and just for a moment, I swore I saw a twinkling in his eye.

Mack put Jud in a half-nelson. Jud slapped at Mack's immense forearm fleetingly, his face growing red from the effort and lack of oxygen to his brain. Martin still tried to land punches, but his pugilistic attempts were in vain as Mack swished Jud from side to side. Once Jud went limp, his eyes disappearing to the whites, Mack let him slide to the polished floor.

Martin, in all his drunken glory, tried to charge Mack. I don't know if the man's blurry vision had led him to believe Mack was now Jud, or just another worthy opponent, but Mack wasn't having a bit of it. Mack came in quickly while Martin approached awkwardly. Snapping his head forward, Mack caught the drunk across the bridge of the nose with his forehead. The man's face seemed to explode in torrents of blood, the most I'd ever seen. Martin wilted like a flower, collapsing to the floor.

The crowd went crazy with applause. Old Hap even stepped in to shake Mack's hand and congratulate him on another job well done. "See, folks, these are the very capable hands I leave you in!"

For the first time that night, through the gore that covered his face, Mack Larson smiled.

IV

After going down Lime and turning left onto Hibiscus, Officer Mack finally stopped in the middle of the road between our houses. Eddy massaged the goose egg sprouting on his forehead while I twiddled my thumbs and watched Mack's eyes in the rearview mirror. They darted back and forth between Eddie and me, the eyes of a cuckoo clock owl.

Finally, Mack spoke. "What to do? What to do?" Then, that smile slowly played over his face, the same one I'd seen the day Bay's End sent Old Hap Carringer off with a bang. A look of amusement crept over his face and made me forget about the scar on his cheek. It hummed, that smile did. It sang that everything was right with the world, even though I knew good and well it wasn't.

Officer Mack nodded at me as if to say it was my turn for something. Then, in one fluid movement, he threw open his car door and stepped out into the night. Through the open driver's side door, I heard the *clop, clop, clop* of his hard-soled shoes on the pavement as he went around the front of the cruiser. Tilting into the turn like a dancer, he rounded the fender and came up to Eddy's door, whistling. The passenger door popped open, and Mack's large torso filled the void.

"Time to go, son," Mack said as he scooped Eddy up in his arms like a newborn baby.

"Eddy," I said weakly, knowing I was helpless to do anything if Mack decided he wasn't done with my friend for the night.

Mack set Eddy down on his feet. Eddy just stared at Mack, seemingly waiting for round two.

"Well, go on," Mack told him.

Eddy didn't hesitate, not for a second. He bolted through the cast of the sodium vapors of the streetlights and cut diagonally across his yard to the side of his house, disappearing around the corner. I only hoped no one was up waiting on him. If Officer Mack really was letting us go with just Eddy's beating and me being scared senseless, then that would have been great. Somehow, though, I doubted it. I just knew it was all too good to be true.

Clop, clop, clop went Mack's shoes as he came back around to my side. My door came open with a rush of wheezing air. Mack waved me out, but I was frozen in place. I tried; I really did. I tried twice in fact, but my body just wouldn't move.

Mack eyed me coldly. "You coming, Franklin?"

"I'm trying," was all I could think to say. My body wouldn't move, no matter how much I willed it. I sat there paralyzed, a deer in Mack Larson's headlights.

Sighing loudly, Mack leaned in, grabbed me under the left arm, and hauled me out of the squad car. He laughed snidely as he slammed the rear door and slid back behind the steering wheel. He slammed the driver's door and I heard the soft electronic humming motor as he rolled down the window.

"I suggest you run, son," Mack said, winking.

"Huh?" I choked.

"I suggest you run. And fast." His hand played over the dashboard, and the night exploded into red and blue flashing lights. I slapped my hands to my ears as the cruiser's siren about deafened me. All up and down the block, windows began to brighten as neighbors awoke to the screeching cacophony coming from the cruiser.

"Say hi to the folks for me," Mack added before speeding away, peeling rubber.

I ran. Not because Mack had told me to, but because I knew I was running out of time. My parents' room was at the front of the house, and I watched in sheer terror as their bedroom light flickered on.

Pushing with everything I had, I slid into the turn around the back of the house. Pedaling hard, I rushed to my window, collapsing against the wall when I finally reached it.

I pried my fingers into the small slit between the window and the sill even as I heard the final wail of Mack's siren in the distance. My fingertips burned with the pressure, and my knuckles threatened to give as I began to make progress. I slid the window further and further, begging, pleading, praying I was in time. Once it was open wide enough, I settled my palms on the sill and hefted my torso up into the opening. As I did so, light from the hallway seeped in under my bedroom door. My pulse hammered in my temples as I struggled inside and flopped down on the floor of my room.

"Trey?" my father called. "You all right in there?"

I didn't answer. I kicked off my shoes and tossed them into the closet. The soft thud of one of them hitting the back wall made me cringe. I tore off my shirt, up and over my head, then flung it into the closet, also. With absolutely no time for my socks and pants, hoping no one would notice, I threw myself into my pajama shirt and dove for the bed. Pillows flew everywhere as I struggled to get my body-double out of the way and me in its place.

Just as I pulled the covers up and over my jeans, Dad opened my door and stuck in his head. The breath I had been holding came out in a mock snore as I screwed my eyelids shut. I whistled a little as I sucked more air.

My father laughed. "He's dead to the world in here," he called back to my mother.

"He'd sleep through the rapture, that kid," my mother hollered back.

My forehead was slick with sweat, and I was already starting to perspire through my nightshirt. I could hear my father's voice further down the hall; he was more than likely back in his room. Believing it was safe, I opened my eyes and saw the light under my bedroom door was gone. Inky black surrounded me. I sighed in relief. I was safe.

Officer Mack, the Westerns, and even my new buddy Eddy were all behind me. I lay for some time, wondering what might have happened if I'd been caught. What exactly would I have said? Certainly, I'd never see Eddy again, and I had already decided I wasn't going to let that happen.

We were going to be all right. I just knew it. I thoroughly believed it. Nothing in the world could come between us, not then, not ever.

Chapter Three: Candy

I

July 2ⁿᵈ, 1992

The saddest part of a first love is that we're all so sure it will never end. Even at the tender age of twelve, love is an ideal, a place just out of reach. We don't really know ourselves at that age, and in turn, can never really know anyone else. It isn't until we've grown old and tired that we realize we've all been, figuratively speaking, in the dark.

Looking back on all this now, it's the abstract bullshit that I remember the most. The smell of raspberry body wash, the lingering touch that sent goosebumps rippling up my arm like a stone in a still pond, the taste of cherry lip gloss, a pair of eyes that never really looked into mine, but through them. That's what I remember about Candice Waters, or as I referred to her, Candy.

The morning after Eddy's introduction to Officer Mack, Dad was in the backyard harvesting Mom's tomato plants, and Mom was doing the dishes after a breakfast of fried Spam and eggs, when I heard the pounding of someone knocking on the front door. I erupted from my room where I had been folding laundry, just knowing it had to be Eddy. I stormed through the house in a full sprint, hollering, "I got it!" the entire way as I traversed the halls like an Indy car driver.

The girl positively glowed. Her hair was purple-black in the rays of the sun peeking in from under our porch roof. The smile on her face held some of the straightest teeth I'd ever seen. Those hazel eyes swam into me like a practiced diver; they went down deep to the very pit of my being. I felt a stirring in my jeans—something I'd just started to notice recently—and I knew what was coming. The stiffening made me yearn for a little privacy and a dimly lit bathroom.

"Can, uh… can I help you?" Suave, I was not.

"Hey, Trey." She giggled, and the laughter brought me back to reality.

I laughed. "Hey-o, Candice." I knew her; of course, I did. We walked home together every day when school was in session. I fought for why I hadn't recognized her, but the reason eluded me.

"You look… different," was all I could manage.

"Makeup. Dad finally gave into me and Mom's constant nagging, and he started letting me wear it." I could see her blush even under her foundation. "I've been staying with him a lot since the breakup. Probably the reason I look… different."

"You look great!" It just burst out of me. I really had no control over my mouth at that precise moment. "You look like a girl!"

That last line made me see what I hadn't seen before. Candice Waters did, in fact, look like a girl. Every other time I'd seen her, she had been in a T-shirt and jeans, flip flops or sandals, and with her hair in a ponytail or under a baseball cap. I had never seen the Candice at my door.

It was much more than just makeup, too.

Candy had blossomed nicely. Two peaks pushed at the chest of her form-fitting silk blouse—I just assumed it was silk, because it looked like it would have been nice and soft if I touched it—coming to sharp points that seemed to threaten blindness if I got too close. Her nipples were hard, pressing against the soft fabric, asking for an audience. And she had *curves*. She might have had them all along, but I wouldn't have noticed in her usual attire of loose, baggy boy clothes. That may have been the reason I missed the slow growth of her chest, as well.

"Well, sheesh, thanks, I guess."

"Huh?" I asked as I finally met her eyes again.

"Never mind." She giggled. "Is your mom home?"

"Duh-yeah," I stammered. "Why?"

"I'm selling Avon for my mom. She works at the hospital with your mom, and she thought that your mom would like to buy some. They're on different shifts now, so, you know."

"Yeah, uh... sure." I opened the door further. "Come on in. She's just cleaning up from breakfast."

I watched her walk past me into the foyer and noticed even the way she walked had changed. Her hips swung from side to side, each butt cheek lifting and dropping, lifting and dropping. It was certainly a sight to behold, and I was praying for the privacy of that bathroom as something pushed hard against the inside of my zipper.

"Mom!" I called out without taking my eyes off of Candice's rump. "You got company!"

Candice ducked and clapped a hand to the side of her head. I wondered why, before realizing I had just yelled in her ear.

"Sorry," I hissed as I sucked air through my teeth.

She laughed. "S'okay, I guess." She shook her head.

"They ringing?"

"What?"

"Are your ears ringing?" I yelled, not really intending to, but doing it all the same.

"They are now!" she screamed back.

We stood there for a moment, sharing something in each other's eyes, completely silent. The rest of the world was devoid of life at that very second. There was only her and me in that foyer, staring, accepting something that seemed to have been forever coming. I forgot about Mom, Dad, didn't care to think about Eddy or Officer Mack, because in truth, none of them existed. Not while we were there, hidden where only hearts could find us.

"Hello, Candice," Mom said, breaking our trance. Candice smiled at me, and I returned it before she spun around and approached my mother.

"Hello, Mrs. Franklin. How are you doing?"

"I'm fine, Candice. And you?"

"Perfect, thank you. My mom wants to know if you want to buy some Avon."

"Sure." Mom stopped with her mouth open as if she wanted to say something else, but the sight of me standing in the foyer stopped her. She stared at me, mouth agape, cheeks reddening, as she looked from my eyes to my crotch. Eyes, crotch.

"Candice," Mom finally said, still not taking her eyes off me. "Will you go lay everything out on the kitchen table for me?"

"Sure thing, Mrs. Franklin," Candice said as she walked off out of view.

"I'll be right there, sweetie. Just lay everything out for me," Mom called in a singsong voice. Then to me, she hissed, "Trey Franklin!"

"What?" I asked, confused.

"Go take care of that." She pointed at my pants.

I looked down and thought my world would end right then and there.

Jutting from my crotch was a tent on the front of my jeans. It stood quite proud, as if I had a balled up sock shoved down the front of my pants. I could feel it throbbing. Mom stared at it, wide-eyed, as she motioned for me to leave, mouthing "hurry." I felt my face flush, and my mouth went dry. I disappeared down the hallway, my manhood rubbing hard against the inside of my jeans.

As I burst through the bathroom door, I ejaculated. I doubled over, bending my knees as wave after wave of pure pleasure throttled me. Straightening, I saw the brain-damaged look on my face in the bathroom mirror. I felt something warm slithering down the inside of my leg, like a sunbaked worm.

Once I composed myself, I dropped my pants and cleaned. My penis was so tender to the touch I almost screamed as the wet, tacky washcloth scrubbed away my semen. I knew what had happened; I'd taken sex education, but that made it no less of a shock.

To this day, I don't know if Candy noticed my impromptu salute to her. I would like to say that she didn't, but I'm more apt to believe she just never mentioned it.

Mom played it off well and ended up buying a hundred dollars' worth of Avon from Candy. I don't know if Mom was just trying to buy me some time, or if she really wanted the items, but I silently thanked her for that.

II

Closer to the noon side of the day, Eddy finally showed up on my doorstep. Candice was two hours gone, and Eddy was a sight for sore eyes. When I opened the door, Eddy almost ran me over to get inside.

"I just saw the hottest chick walking down the block, man. Whew, a fucking scorcher," Eddy said as he stood in the foyer adjusting the front of his pants.

"You mean Candice?" I asked, unable to keep from laughing at him.

"Whoever, man. She was grade-A, prime chuck, like the old man says. Can we go to your room? Got something to show you." He looked from left to right.

"Yeah, sure. Come on." I led him down the hallway.

My bedroom was that of a typical twelve-year-old boy. I had a dresser stuffed with clothes I still wore, but had mostly outgrown. My parents were still under the impression I might have a little brother one day and refused to give up the things to Goodwill. Stacks of cardboard boxes filled to the brim with thousands of baseball cards sat in one corner next to my closet. My entertainment center with a nineteen-inch television and Sega Genesis was the most prominent thing in my room. Eddy skirted all of it so he could hop up and crash down onto my bed.

"Fucking comfy shit, man."

"Dude," I growled. "Language?"

"Oh, yeah." He shrugged. "Sorry. I forget not everyone's parents are as loose as mine."

"Really, dude? Shoes?" I pointed to the mess he was making of my sheets with his dirt-clogged soles.

"Damn, you're picky!" He flipped me off as he swung his legs around and sat on the edge.

His 'tits or tires' shirt was gone, replaced with one that read, "I'm a handyman! Lemme see your pipes!" I had to laugh inwardly when I read it. I just hoped Mom wouldn't see it. If she did, we'd have to play the explanation game, and I didn't feel like it. He wore a different pair of jeans, but they were just as holey as the ones from the previous day. His white-and-red striped K-Swiss sneakers had seen better days, but so had every single pair of kicks in my closet.

"Whatcha wanna show me?" I asked as I sat beside him on the bed.

"This, of course." Eddy flashed me his bucks as he pulled a handful of round red balls from his pocket. Each one had the telltale gray fuse sticking out of them that just screamed, "Cherry bombs!"

My eyes shot open like high beams, and I snatched one out of his hand. "For real!"

"I was thinking about firing them off out at the Westerns. Whatcha say?"

"Are you fucking crazy?" I almost screamed. I clapped a hand over my mouth, hoping I wouldn't hear my mom stomping down the hall toward my room, a belt cutting the air around her.

"Man, come on. That pussy-ass cop ain't going to be out there again. He just busted us last night, and the asshole's last thought will be that we'd go right back. Right?"

"I don't know." I handed him the firecracker. "What if he's out there, for real? You know it won't be pretty, dude."

"Lemme handle it if he shows up." Eddy shot me those buck teeth.

"Yeah. 'Cause you handled it so well last night."

"Fuck you." He rubbed the knot on his forehead and cringed. "Dad said he'd have the dude's job if he ever came at me like that again."

"Wait," I said, shocked. "You told your dad what happened?"

"And my mom. That cock knocker won't pull that shit again. Betcha! My dad will have his fucking nuts in a sling."

"They weren't mad?"

"They never are when I tell them the truth. It's all about me being honest with them. Shit, they mighta let me go out last night if I'd asked them. But where's the fun in that?" He elbowed me in the bicep.

I rubbed my arm. "Wish I had parents like that."

"So, you coming?"

"I guess so." I shrugged. "What could it hurt?"

"Not a damn thing!" Eddy bounded off my bed and spun in a circle. "Give me explosions… or gimme death!"

"I hope not." I laughed as I stood. Then, a thought occurred to me. "Hey, you wanna see if Candice wants to come?"

"The chick in the skirt?"

"Yeah, why not?"

"No 'why not?' about it, man. I'm game."

"Cool. Which way was she headed when you saw her?"

"Down toward Lime."

"Cool. She was probably on her way home then." I rushed for the door.

I could hear Eddy following as I yelled to my mom where we were heading. She answered from the kitchen, kind of distantly telling me to be safe. I thought about the cherry bombs in Eddy's pocket and chuckled.

"Will do!" I hollered as he and I ran out the front door and took off for Candy's house.

III

The three of us fully intended on going to the Westerns that afternoon. We just never made it.

Candy's mom was asleep. Her mother had to work that night, so Candy just left a note on the fridge. I asked her if she was sure it was cool, and she promised me it was. The last thing I wanted was Ms. Waters being angry with me, especially since I was suddenly so fond of her blooming daughter.

Candy's parents had been separated for more than a year, but her mom, Carrie, had kept her husband's last name. From what I was told, it had been a clean break.

"This stuff just happens," Candy had told me one day on our way home from school. She looked sad, but resolute, as if she knew there was nothing anyone could do about it and it truly was no one's fault. Candy was a hell of a smart kid, and I envied that about her. If I loved Eddy's courage, I was in awe of Candy's intelligence. I always wondered what they saw in me, though.

Things had been a lot simpler when Candy was just one of the guys. With my new feelings, it was hard not to make up a reason for falling behind so I could stare at her butt while she walked. She'd changed into a pair of form-fitting jeans and a tight yellow T-shirt before joining us outside. Gone was the skirt and blouse, but that didn't really matter. She still looked great.

Eddy couldn't keep his eyes off her either, and the thought made me feel weird inside. He walked backward in front of Candy, looking her up and down as though she were naked or something. Eddy was a brash guy, but he was jovial and playful. Candy laughed at him constantly as we made our way to Rifle Park, shooting the shit.

I guess what I was feeling were the first tinges of jealousy. Sure, I'd felt jealous of people before, but never over another human being. I'd coveted toys and baseball cards and even the new bike Dylon Trundell got for his fourteenth birthday just before summer break—damn, but that thing was sweet!—yet I'd never cared about someone who wasn't family enough to be upset that they might like someone else. Hearing Candy laughing at Eddy's goofy ass felt like a steel nail being driven into my gut over and over again, making my heart hammer quicker in my chest.

That feeling didn't last long because my heart completely stopped when we reached Main Street.

Officer Mack Larson had pulled over a blue sedan on the outer edge of Rifle Park. I saw him well before Eddy did because the fool was still walking backward when we left Sequoia. I met Eddy's eyes and jerked my chin in Mack's direction so he'd look that way. We all grew quiet, even Candy for some reason, and stopped on the corner of Sequoia and Main to watch.

Mack was bent over the driver's window of the sedan with his notepad open, writing. The blond woman behind the wheel was visually and audibly upset. I heard her crying and could tell she was begging Mack for leniency. Her hands were clasped together in front of her and moving back and forth as if she were in a fit of prayer.

"... please... my license... revoked... my father..." We were too far away to hear everything, but close enough to catch what was going on.

Mack, on the other hand, spoke plenty loud and clear as a bell. "I'm still going to write you a ticket, ma'am."

"I'll lose... father... I have to drive..."

"Not my concern. You shouldn't have been speeding," Mack said sternly.

"... wasn't... never speed... please..."

"Pssst!" Eddy hissed, getting my attention. He held out an open palm with a lighter and a cherry bomb sitting in the middle of it.

My eyes widened. I shook my head and mouthed, "No way."

"Asshole." Candy glared in Mack's direction. "Do it."

"What?" I hissed. "Are you guys crazy? He'll have our asses for dinner."

"What about what he did to Sanders?" Candy asked, meeting my eyes. Hers looked so sad I almost melted. "You know he called me after Mack took him home after all those windows got broke over at the Westerns."

"Yeah," I whispered. "He called me, too. I feel sorry for Sanders, really, I do. But that..." I pointed at the cherry bombs. "That's just suicide by cop."

"Grow a pair," Eddy chided.

"And what do I do after I grow a pair? Go to jail? I think I'll take verbal castration over whatever you have in mind."

"He just watched Sulan beat Sanders, Trey," Candy said. "He just... smiled."

"I know." I sighed and ran a hand through my hair. "I don't know," I finally said. "What do you wanna do, Eddy?"

"Light up his fucking car, is what I wanna do. Damn right I do." Eddy puffed out his chest and seemed to swell a good six inches taller.

"And then what?" I asked.

"Then, we run." Candy looked into my eyes; she blinked once, then twice, and I knew I wasn't going to win. Hell, with her looking at me like that, I didn't *want* to win.

"We do this right, Trey, and this asshole doesn't even know we're the ones who did it," Eddy assured me. "We sneak up behind the car while he's busy with that lady, light a couple of these bad boys, toss them in through the open window, then take off into the woods. How about that?"

"Sounds good to me," Candy said.

"Fine." I sighed. "Let's get this over with."

IV

The thought occurred to me that the cherry bomb was a horrible idea, but I was along for the ride nonetheless. I didn't know if the reason I gave in could completely be blamed for the way Candy had looked at me because, deep down, I felt something like that should have been done ages ago, but I still felt bad about the outcome.

We made our way across Main Street completely unnoticed. Mack was so involved with the lady in the blue sedan and her insistent bawling that he never looked up from her open window. I shuddered to think he was enjoying himself, loving every minute of the torture.

Candy snuck off into Rifle Park and hid behind a tree—remember, she was the smart one—while Eddy and I crouched behind the cruiser's trunk. I watched Mack from around the side of the car while Eddy prepared his munitions. I thought at the time he was only going to use one of the firecrackers, but he ended up with all four in his hand by the time he was ready to make his move.

Eddy dipped low and crouch-walked, staying tight with the side of the cruiser. I heard the police radio squawking about a lost dog having been found on the corner of Fern and Oak, and I automatically recognized the voice of Jenna Wales, the dispatcher.

I watched as Eddy found his way under the rear driver-side door. His hand went for the handle, and I cringed. I had expected him just to light the things and toss them in through the open window, but apparently, he had a better idea. He produced a pocketknife from his back pocket as he opened the door. From what I could tell, he was cutting up the upholstery of the driver's seat. He worked quickly, the hand with the knife steadily disappearing and reappearing in and out of the opening. Finally, he twisted the cherry bomb wicks together, lit them, and stuffed them into the seat. I barely heard the soft popping and sizzling over Jenna's voice coming out of the radio. The next thing I knew, Eddy was coming around me, heading for the tree line.

In hindsight, I'm kind of glad Eddy opened the car door. It gave us plenty of time to escape without being seen.

The three of us were about fifty yards into the woods that surrounded Rifle Park when the commotion began. We ran as if the devil was on our heels. The first of the cherries went off with a *Boom!* that sounded like gunfire, and I had reels of war movies playing in my mind's eye as we advanced further into the trees.

Candy led us off on a pathway I hadn't seen in ages. The trail wasn't like the main stone one that led through the park, nor was it like High Stone. It was nothing but a beaten path kids had created and explored over the years. I knew where it led and a funny feeling hit my stomach, one of excitement.

The second bomb went off, followed by the third, and the sounds sent us into fits of laughter. I was having the most fun I'd had in ages, and I never wanted it to stop. I couldn't understand, not at that moment, why in the world I hadn't wanted to do it. It was just amazing. The part I never got to see, but wished to God I had, was the look on Mack's face as he watched in horror while his driver's seat exploded over and over again. I could imagine the blond lady smiling through her tears, silently thanking whoever had given her that sweet revenge. In my mind, I fantasized that Mack stood in the middle of Main Street, scratching his disfigured cheek and ruminating on the hows and whys of the situation.

A fourth bomb went off, followed by a fifth.

"What was that?" Eddy asked, no longer laughing.

"What was what?" I asked, struggling to run and talk at the same time.

"That last one... didn't sound the same... did it?" Eddy wheezed.

"Fuck if... I know."

"Just shut up and run!" Candy called from ahead of us as a sixth *Boom!* echoed.

V

Candy was leading us to Hunter's Point, and I couldn't wait. The woods grew thicker as we left the outer edge of Rifle Park and delved deeper into the lesser known reaches of The End's outskirts. If the Westerns were on the west edge of The End, then Hunter's Point was at the northern tip. It wasn't much, really, just a make-out spot for the older teenagers and a car park for the hunters who gathered up there in the fall months, but the view of The End was amazing.

From the highest section of Hunter's Point, you could see the entire town. Bachman High and Nettles Middle School were off to the south. Young Elementary was even further south, but we couldn't see it from Hunter's Point. Peaton's Grocery sat at the heart of The End, right across from City Hall, where Chief Hap had held his retirement party. To the east was the radio station where Stewart Berkin played oldies nonstop and the fairgrounds where Bay's End held an annual carnival.

We crested the top of Hunter's Point, completely out of breath, and collapsed to the gravel as we fought to regain our composure. Eddy rolled back and forth on his back, laughing hard again, even as he tried to calm down from the run.

One moment, I was looking up at pure blue sky, not a cloud in sight, then suddenly I was face to face with Candy and her beautiful hazels. My breath hitched, and I flinched a little as she moved to straddle me.

"You gonna be all right, Trey?" She tossed her head back, her chest heaving from the exertion.

"Yeah... why?" I asked in between breaths.

"You seemed a little hesitant back there, Franklin," Eddy said.

"What he said," she told me, smiling with those perfect teeth of hers.

"Come on, give me a break. I was just being rational," I wheezed. It was getting harder to breathe with Candy sitting on me, but I wasn't about to tell her to move.

"Rational, huh?" Candy asked.

"Yeah, what's wrong with being rational?"

"If everything in this world was rational, would I be able to do this?"

She kissed me.

"Whoop!" Eddy burst from beside us, but he soon melted away.

My mouth was flooded with tongue and the taste of cherry lip gloss. Candy seemed to be hunting something back by my molars as she played around in there, traveling deeper and deeper, until I thought she would soon make her way down my throat. I grasped the back of her head and pulled her even closer. Her hair fell around me and cast a shade on the day, like our own private room away from the world. The smell of raspberry shampoo filled my nose, mixing with the cherry gloss and making me think of pie. She retreated, licking my upper lip as she went. When I finally opened my eyes again, not realizing I had closed them, she was smiling coyly.

Eddy laughed again. "Now, that was a fucking kiss. Whoop!"

"All better?" Candy asked, wiping her lips with a thumb and forefinger.

"What was that for?" I asked, blinking wildly.

"Just 'cause." She leaned in and kissed my cheek. "See what a little irrationality will get you in life?"

"I could learn to be irrational."

"Really now?" She tucked her hair behind her ears as she straightened to a sitting position.

"Bet you could!" Eddy reeled, holding his gut while he laughed.

I smiled. "Might be fun."

"Might just." She kissed her index and middle fingers and slapped them on my forehead. "What now?" she asked as she turned to face Eddy.

"Your show, boss," Eddy told her.

"This was your show just a minute ago." She suddenly looked confused. "What's your name, by the way?"

The entire time, everything we'd been through so far that day, and I hadn't even introduced them.

"That's Eddy Treemont. This is Candice Waters." I pointed at each one as I said their respective names.

Candy nodded at him. "Nice to meet you, Eddy."

"Fuck you very much, Candice." Eddy flipped her off.

"Well, aren't you the gentleman?"

"Not quite." Eddy chuckled. "Highly fucking unlikely, Candy Cane."

She smirked. "It's Candice, short rod."

"Well, excuse me, Mrs. Candice, ma'am."

"I should say you're not excused, douchebag." She stuck her tongue out at him.

"Save the tongue for tonsil-hockey with Romeo over there. You're not my type."

"Oh, yeah? Why? 'Cause I have a pulse?"

We stayed at Hunter's Point until the sun threatened to go down. We heard sirens in the distance, but thought nothing of it. We were sure we hadn't been seen because, if we had, there would have been cops all over us. As the daylight waned, we grew tired of sitting around and conversing, and decided to head back home.

Candy and I walked hand in hand, while Eddy walked with his in his pockets. We talked about school and how it would suck to go back. Then we discussed how Eddy would fit in with the other kids around town in the coming months and years. Candy talked about how she hated her mom being on the graveyard shift because she never saw her anymore. I told them about how Mom wanted me to get a scholarship to some big school, but that Dad would prefer I played for those inept Cubs of his. We talked because that was what we did best. It was real. It was full of life and struggle and failures and wins, but most of all, it was *us*. We were getting to know each other, really getting to know each other. At that moment, I couldn't have wanted to be anywhere else in the world, at any other time. I just wanted to be right there, with my friends, walking through The End as though we didn't have a care in the world.

Interlude 2: Skeletons in the Closet

Back here for a moment, while I gather my thoughts.

It seems the ghost in my closet is growing restless. I keep having to stop writing to check the padlock on the door. I can hear it growling in there, begging for release. I just don't know if I can relive that yet.

Eddy has been watching me write from his place on the edge of the bed. He hasn't aged a day. Every now and again, I see him push his wire rims further up the bridge of his nose and flash me those bucks. The sight makes my heart hurt. He keeps motioning toward the closet, but I'm pretending to ignore him.

What lies in wait behind that closet door has held a greater power over me than anything else in my entire life. Letting it out now doesn't seem like that great of an idea. I feel that I must, though. If Eddy thinks it's a good idea, then maybe I should take his advice.

I can feel a sense of closure coming from all of this. Even now, Eddy is starting to dim. He's not as there as he was when I started this diatribe. I can feel him burning out like a dying star, feel him leaving. That, if for no other reason, is why I'm pressing on.

The ghost in the closet is calling, and it can no longer wait. I'm afraid Eddy is just going to have to be patient. Just a few more miles to go, old soul... a few more miles.

Chapter Four: Sanders

I

July 6ᵗʰ, 1992

Xingchin Sanderson threw open the door of his house like a prisoner escaping his bonds. His long black hair streamed behind him like the flags of the Bachman High Color Guard. His smile stretched from the point of each squinted eye to the other. He was bubbly, something I'd never seen him be, and Candy chuffed as he slammed into her, embracing her in an all-encompassing hug of companionship.

"I'm free!" he belted, and I saw Candy pull away as his voice filled her fragile ear canal. I had last seen him only three weeks before, but his normal caramel-colored skin looked lighter from lack of sun. He got his color from his mother, but his features were completely Asian, like his father. Tony Marchesini called Sanders "Half-Breed" not only for the obvious reason, but also because his long jet-black mane made him look like a warrior Comanche.

"How the fudge are you, Trey?" Sanders asked as he released his hold on Candy and slapped five with me. His brown eyes shimmered, and I once again thought of a recently paroled inmate happy to be on the outside.

I laughed. "How the fudge are *you*?"

Sanders didn't cuss. He didn't have the control I had, or the understanding parents that Eddy possessed, so we had to be careful not to fully corrupt him.

Eddy cleared his throat, and the rest of us turned to see him standing there with his hands deep in his pockets. Four days had passed since he'd cherry-bombed Officer Mack's cruiser, and he had been waiting to meet Sanders and give him the good news.

"Who the hell is this?"

Kids are rude, but they're also curious. Sanders proved both of those statements as his eyes played over Eddy's short form.

"This little bastard is Eddy Treemont," I said.

"He cool?" Sanders asked as if Eddy weren't even there.

"On occasion." I smiled.

"Fuck you, Trey." Eddy cocked his chin at me.

"You wanna tell him? Or should we?" Candy asked Eddy.

"I'm the one who did it, ain't I?" Eddy responded.

"Did what?" Sanders asked.

"Did you hear about Officer Mack's cruiser last Sunday?" Eddy asked.

"The cherries?" Sanders eyes grew wide. "Everyone around town is talking about it!"

"Yeah," Eddy said. "Well, that was all me."

"Frigging amazing!"

"Not entirely you," I said.

"All you did was watch out," Eddy scoffed.

"That was plenty help, though," Candy said.

"Wait, wait, wait." Sanders waved his hand in front of his face as if he smelled something bad. "You had something to do with bombing Officer

Mack Larson's patrol car? *You* never do *anything*!" He directed that little bit at me.

"I have noticed… Trey is kind of a pussy." Eddy laughed.

"You can say that again," Sanders added, smiling at me.

"Guys, come on," Candy interjected. "Trey's the reason we're all friends now." She grabbed my hand and kissed me on the cheek. I felt electricity shoot through me, and I begged my member to behave. Candy and I had gotten quite close over the past couple of days, and I saw the surprise in Sanders's eyes.

"No way," Sanders huffed. "You two a thing now?"

"Could say that." I smiled.

"Bullcrap, Trey." Sanders grabbed Candy's forearm playfully and swung her over to him. "You're mine, chick."

"Who says?" Candy giggled.

"The gods say."

"Whatever! Always the ever-dreaming geek," she said. "Glad to see jail time hasn't changed you, Sanders."

"Thy will be done. Kiss me, wench!"

Sanders leaned in to lay one on her. Candy spun out of his grasp and took off toward Main

Street at a full sprint. Sanders smiled, his eyes squinting tighter. He rocketed after her. I looked at Eddy, Eddy looked at me, and I shrugged.

Eddy sighed. "You guys are fucking weird."

"Welcome to my world."

Just before we both took off, I caught something out of the corner of my eye. Romo paced back and forth in his runner, oddly quiet given that the four of us had had our little reunion in Sanders's front yard. The white wolf didn't make a sound; he just stared. The way that mutt looked at me, the new patience in his eyes, seemed odd, making my stomach churn.

I couldn't help but be reminded of Mack Larson at Hap Carringer's retirement party.

Not watching.

Waiting.

II

We ended up at Chapman's Laundromat that afternoon, pumping quarters into the new Mortal Kombat box they'd installed in the back next to Cruis'n USA. The game was challenging, and we played for three hours, swapping turns each time a new opponent handed us our asses.

Goro, the final boss, came onto the screen, flexing all four of his arms, and we gawked at the screen as if it held the meaning of life. When he ripped Sanders's character, Sub-Zero, apart with a flawless victory, we all decided the game had stolen enough of our money for one day.

"I could've kept playing, you know," Eddy moped as we made our way back out into the high afternoon sun.

"Dude," I said. "It's almost three o'clock, and I don't feel like wasting my time inside all day."

"You guys wanna go to the Westerns?" Sanders asked. The question made us all stop.

"You just, and I mean just three hours ago, got off restriction because of all those windows you broke, and you wanna go back there?" Candy asked incredulously.

"Why the heck not? It's not like I'm gonna start throwing rocks again." Sanders placed a hand over his heart and his other up in a boy scout's three-fingered pledge. "I'm a reformed man, Boss."

We all laughed.

"If you really want to." I shrugged.

"Guys?" Eddy wheezed in a hushed voice.

"Yeah?" I asked, coming up alongside him. He was facing the glass storefront of Harper's Fine Goods, next door to the laundromat, and frowning. I followed his gaze to the posted bill in the window.

"Emily Harper," I read. "Age twenty-two, of 119 French Street, Bay's End, has been missing since July second."

"That was the day Eddy taught Mack his lesson." Candy pointed out.

"Emily was last seen leaving her house in her blue Honda Civic by a neighbor..."

"Sounds like the car—"

Candy cut Eddy off. "Shush."

"If you have any information, please contact Bay's End Police Department, Extension 57. Ask for—"

"Officer Mack Larson," Eddy finished. "Trey, is that...?"

"It sure as hell looks like her," I replied, my voice cracking.

The picture behind the glass showed a pretty blond-haired woman. Emily Harper smiled at us from that photo of days past with the sun on her shoulders and what looked to be her house in the background. She was petting a brown dog.

"She's missing?" Candy finally said, breaking the silence that had crashed down like a tangible entity.

"Been missing since Sunday." I didn't know why I whispered.

"That was the day..." Eddy put his hand to his mouth.

"Can't have anything to do with that, nimrod." Candy laughed, but I could hear the nervousness there, the fear.

"Come on, let's get outta here." Eddy turned away from the window. "I don't wanna think about this shit."

I laughed softly, pressing Emily Harper to the back of my mind. "Yeah, me neither."

"Where to now?" Sanders asked.

"Still wanna hit the Westerns?"

"Nah." Sanders, who had not been a part of our little bombing run and didn't know who Emily Harper might have been, smiled. "What about Bachman High? Stop by my place, grab the balls, bats, and gloves, and get in a game before the sun goes down."

"Awesome!" Eddy erupted. "Didn't know you played! Fucking cool."

"Not only does our friend Sanders play—" I started.

"I'm a fudging god at it," Sanders finished.

We raced away from Harper's Fine Goods and forgot all about Emily's smiling face in that window. There were games to be played and good friends to wear away the day with. We had no time for sad things.

I knew right then I didn't want to be a part of any of it. I'd seen the look of uncertainty in Eddy's eyes and the nervousness in Candy's. We all knew that Eddy had only had four cherry bombs that day, but there had been six explosions. And even though the math didn't added up, we'd never thought another thing about it.

I now miss that childhood innocence, that blissful ignorance that told me it wasn't my fault.

114

Chapter Five: Tony and the Tramps

I

The summer sun was at its pinnacle, and the day had rounded four o'clock by the time we'd picked up the equipment and landed at the high school. Bachman Field was where The Enders played baseball in the spring. They normally had twelve games, but the final game had been canceled that year due to rain and had never been rescheduled. Sanders and I had attended every game. Candy had, too, but she'd always sat with her mom. The Enders sucked almost as bad as Dad's Cubs. They were horrible that last season, more so than usual, but it was still exciting watching all the failed swings and dropped balls, along with the laundry list of errors they'd racked up.

When our group came around the cafeteria, located in the central area of Bachman High, we couldn't help but hang our heads. Tony and the Tramps, consisting of Tony Marchesini, Willy Dubose, Nathan Flemming, and Greg Wallace, were playing their own game and looked to be in a heated battle.

Tony was a self-obsessed kid at the best of times and a holy terror at the worst of them. All four of those guys were a year ahead of us in school, aside from Greg who'd been held back a year, and were freshmen at Bachman. Tony was the only one who had actually made The Enders lineup, not because he was any good, though. His mom was 'laying pipe' with Coach Booker, and that piece of ass had landed Tony a spot as right fielder his first year on the team. That little trade was one of the reasons The Enders were so bad that season. Tony couldn't catch herpes from a sore-ridden whore, much less a baseball.

The rest of his goons—the Tramps as my mother called them because of the way they ran the streets causing trouble—weren't quite as bad as Tony, but they weren't angels, either.

Willy Dubose was the second child of Shana and Monty Dubose, who owned Bay's End Inn. His little sister Sissy had been the first girl in the fifth grade to grow a pair of breasts. Willy walked bowlegged, like a cowboy fresh off a long ride and suffering from saddle burn. He was a cocky teen, full of piss and vinegar, and rumor had it, he'd laid it to his neighbor's wife while the husband had been away on business. Gossip like that spread like wildfire in a town as small as ours.

Nathan was a good enough sort, but only because he was the quiet one. He hung out with Tony and the Tramps because they were the "In" crowd. They were the place to be, so to speak. Nathan was also the biggest of the brood. A fourteen-year-old who stood six-foot-something was a force to be reckoned with, and I always assumed that was why he never talked. Because, truthfully, he didn't have to.

Greg was the lame duck of the group, and I felt sorry for him, mostly. Greg was a fifteen-year-old eighth grader who would probably never see a graduation stage. He'd been held back in the second grade because he couldn't spell his own name. Sad, really, considering his name only consisted of four letters. I'd blame his parents, but I didn't know them.

Tony was pitching and in mid-windup when he spotted us. I knew from the look in his eyes and the smile that slowly crept across his face that the high school horror would want to play us.

Willy, who was at bat, yelled at Tony to "Fucking pitch the goddamn ball, ass clown."

Tony pointed at us. Willy turned his head, his face twisting into a grin when he saw us. Greg and Nathan jogged in from the field.

"What the holy hell we got here?" Tony asked as he spit onto the clay strip that led to first base.

"We got ourselves some practice dummies," Willy mused, imitating his illustrious leader by spitting, also.

"We don't want any trouble, guys," Sanders said meekly. He kept his gaze trained on Tony's feet.

"What the fuck, Half-Breed? You too good to play with the likes of us?" Tony hitched a thumb at Greg. "We're handicapped 'cause of Goofy Gregory over here."

"One game wouldn't hurt," Eddy said. Candy, Sanders, and I snapped our heads around at the same time to look at him.

Willy glared at Eddy. "Who is fucking this?"

"*I'm* fucking Eddy."

I thought back to how he'd back talked Mack and sighed in frustration. Sometimes, I just wished he would shut up.

"New around here?" Greg grumbled.

"Thank you, Captain Obvious. Your powers of observation are out-fucking-standing." Tony clipped Greg in the knee with the end of his bat. The sound that came out of Greg was a mixture of Goofy's trademark Yuck-Yuck and Homer Simpson's "D'oh."

"So," Willy spoke up, "you bastards game or not?"

"We'll play ya," Candy said, sticking out her chin, trying to look confident.

"The little lady speaks!" Tony pointed the bat at her chest. "Nice tits, by the way. Didn't have those last year, did ya?"

"Shut it, Tony," I heard myself say. I didn't mean to. It just sort of came out.

"Touchy, touchy, Trey!" Tony laughed. "You guys got enough gloves?"

"Can you count to four?" Eddy asked. We all raised our leather-fitted catching hands.

"I don't think I like your mouth, asshole." Tony gave Eddy the evil eye and shifted the bat so it pointed to Eddy's face. "Maybe I should shut it for you, eh?"

"I don't like your face," Eddy came back. "But there ain't shit none of us can do about that."

The Tramps, all three of them, found that to be very funny, indeed. Tony snapped his head from side to side, giving them the shut-the-fuck-up look. They did as his eyes told them.

"We playing?" Eddy looked at the rest of our group. We all nodded one at a time.

"Good deal!" Tony bellowed. "Let's play fucking ball."

II

The rules were simple. It was the only way you could play four-on-four baseball and keep it semi-fair.

Each team had a pitcher, two basemen—one between first and second and another between second and third—and an outfielder. Strikes were when you whiffed a swing, hit the ball behind you, or just plain refused to go for it. Balls were when you fouled out, and home runs were anything over the fence. Once the ball was in play, the pitcher would assume the catcher position if anyone was on third or on the verge of making it home. If anyone caught the ball, that team's turn was up.

Easy enough. Just the way we liked it.

Tony and the Tramps took first bat because... well, because they could. We really didn't have a say in the matter, so we just rolled with the punches. I stood on the pitcher's mound, bent over with my ball hand inside my glove, staring Tony down while he rotated his bat through a few practice swings.

"First to five, all right, kids," Tony hollered. It wasn't really a question so much as it was an order from the master himself. Tony stepped back away from the plate and laid his bat on his right shoulder, preparing his stance. "Pitch, fucker!"

I wound up my first pitch and sent it shooting level with his throat. If it were a real game with a catcher and an umpire, it would have been called a clear ball. But since every pitch was a strike whether you swung or not, Tony went for it anyway. The ball clipped his bat just above his hands and went rocketing into space like the Challenger Shuttle. I made to step forward, hoping I could run up and catch it, but decided better of it when I saw where it was headed. The ball landed in a cloud of red clay, and Tony cussed loudly as he waved his right hand in front of him as though it were on fire.

"Careful, dipshit!" he yelled.

"It didn't even hit you, jerkwad!" Eddy called from between first and second. "I've been playing and watching this game long enough to know the sound of a ball hitting wood and one hitting skin."

Tony flipped Eddy off with his supposedly abused hand, and Eddy returned the gesture, only he took off his glove so that he could proudly extend both middle fingers. Tony called him all different kinds of "fuckers and cocksuckers" before picking up the ball and throwing it back to me.

"Strike one!" Sanders yelled from mid-field.

"Two more, Tony," Candy teased, sticking out her tongue.

"Just get ready for it, cunt," Tony growled. "It's coming straight for *you*." He pointed at her.

"Knock the rug off it, Tone!" Greg yelled from the stands while he scratched his junk.

"Just watch the ball," Willy called.

"Shut the fuck up with that shit. Dammit." Tony took his batting stance again. "Pitch it, dickhead!"

I let my second pitch rip with all the curve ball fury I'd practiced over the years, side arming it like the Wild Thing did when he pitched relief for the Cubs. It went wide, wider than I'd hoped, but began to come back in at the end of its trip toward home plate. Tony leaned into his swing. The tip of the bat connected with the ball, causing it to shear off to the right like a speeding train. The ball hit the cage behind the batter, and the chain-link rattled from the impact.

"Strike two, Tony Maroni!" Sanders whistled gleefully.

"One more," Candy counted down.

"Want me to come in there and show you how to hold a bat?" Eddy laughed, doubling over from the effort.

"Just you wait," Tony mumbled as he retrieved the ball and sent it back my way.

I bent at the waist as I sized him up. A solid fastball would do, I thought, as I squeezed the leather in my hand until it crackled against the skin of my palm. Winding up and leaning back, I kicked out my right leg and put all the heat I could into it. It was a bullet, spinning white and red as it zipped toward the strike zone in a perfectly straight line.

To this day, I can hear the sound of that bat connecting with my pretty little fastball, and I think back to the cherry bombs in Mack's cruiser. *Boom!* came a sound like a shotgun blast opening a door. Wood splintered, debris flew, and chips the size of toothpicks rained down over me as I watched the ball sail well over my head.

I spun on my heels as I saw that white meteor high up in the sky, losing it for only the briefest second in the sun before the ball spun out the other side. My gaze followed the white orb in its long slow arc.

Candy and Sanders ran for the outfield in an in-case-shit-happens move, but Sanders was on that ball like white on rice. That lanky boy ran, legs and arms pumping so fast they blurred, not seeming to notice or care that the outfield fence was coming up quick. I cringed, just knowing he was going to cut himself in half on the chain-link fence.

With all the grace of a ballerina, Sanders kicked out his right leg and shoved the toe of his tennis shoe into the links. Pushing, twisting, and pivoting, he used the fence as a launching pad. He shot up into the air another five feet, arm extended, and I watched that tiny white dot disappear into his brown glove.

Tony was already around second by the time I focused back in on him. He slid to a stop, a cloud of clay dust settling around him, when he finally came to terms with what had happened.

"Motherfucker!" Tony exploded. "You gotta be kidding me!"

"Right on, man!" Eddy screamed at Sanders, who was running back to the infield with the ball bouncing up and down in his glove.

"Told you, poop stain. I'm a *god* at this game." Sanders laughed.

"I would say so!" Eddy gave Sanders a high five. Then to Tony, he said, "How you like *that* shit?"

"Watch that fucking mouth. I told you about that fucking mouth," Tony growled.

"Seems someone is a poor sport," Candy said.

Candy was too close to Tony for that comment. She'd come jogging back across the field and was just starting to pass him when she said it. Tony didn't have to do much. He drew back and swung just as hard as he had at my fastball. The slap sent Candy's head snapping to the side, her torso reeling back, and her legs flying from underneath her. Even while she was in midair, I could see the left side of her face flash with a red handprint before she slammed down hard on her back.

"Fucking bitch," Tony hissed. "You better learn your goddamn place."

I could tell you I acted promptly, but I didn't. I'd like to say I stole into battle with a samurai's grace and speed, but I didn't. I would be lying if I said I sprang into action. So, this is what actually went down.

I flat out stumbled. Like Wile E. Coyote going off a cliff, my feet spun, and I staggered forward with all the poetic balance of a punch-drunk boxer. My arm came up to punch, but instead just lightly grazed Tony's back. My right shoulder slid across his back, causing him to turn out of my way, and I plummeted the full five feet, face first, into the clay beside second base.

Tony didn't waste a single second. He drove a kick into my stomach with the force of a special team kicker going for a field goal. My breath escaped in one big *Whoosh!* I felt myself being pulled up into a standing position by the front of my shirt. Then, just as quick, I was on the ground again, only that time, I was on my back. Tony came at me like a raging bull, his chest rising and falling in quick, very upset breaths. I could easily envision steam whistling from his nose and ears while fire licked out of his lips across his Cupid's bow.

"Get up!" he bellowed, just before being tackled out of view.

At first, I didn't have a clue what had happened. I was too busy trying to catch my wind. My chest was working, I could feel it, but my throat wasn't allowing any air in or out. My respiratory system said, "Closed. Come again!" as I struggled to regain some kind of composure.

I rolled onto my side, praying for that first gasp to fill my lungs with life-saving oxygen, but nothing came. What I did see was Sanders helping Candy to her feet as she clutched the left side of her face in her hands. Tears streamed down her cheek from a single bloodshot eye. I couldn't see the other eye because she had her hand over it, but I could imagine what it looked like.

Sanders and Candy came to me. Even with her face fiery red and wet with tears, Candy still knelt by my side and helped me to sit up. She laid a calm hand on my back, while keeping the other at her cheek.

"Breathe," was all she said.

That grateful rush of wind finally came, the one I was sure had left me forever. I swallowed gulp after gulp of glorious oxygen as stars played across my vision, and my ears thrummed with rushing blood. The world was spinning, and everything threatened to go black. I'd been without a good solid breath too long, and with the air flooding in unabated, I felt like a starving kid who had just devoured a Thanksgiving turkey all by himself—full and sick. I coughed hard, too hard for Candy's liking, and she peeled herself off of me, giving me space.

"That's it," she whispered as she rubbed my back.

At the time, I thought what I saw behind the fence in left field was nothing more than just a vision, a mirage. Looking back, I know that I was completely wrong.

Way off in the distance, Romo was walking under the summer sun. The white wolf disappeared around the corner of one of the school buildings, with his tail wagging and his head hung low as he sniffed the ground.

III

When I finally came back to reality, Eddy was straddling Tony and wailing on his face with well-placed lefts and rights. The Tramps were storming in, but having their leader being pummeled right in front of them kind of stole their thunder. Willy, Nathan, and Greg all stood there, like the remaining three of us, shocked that Tony was taking such a beating.

"Motherfuckering..." Punch. "... titty sucking..." Punch. "... two-balled bitch," Eddy sang between blows. He sounded as though he was having a blast throttling Tony. "Your daddy's got a pussy..." Punch. "... and your momma's..."

Punch. "... got a dick." Eddy laughed when he finally pulled himself off of the bloodied older boy. He whipped his hand down to his side and torrents of blood splashed onto the clay. That was going to be a nasty little surprise for the groundskeeper when he came out to get the field ready next season.

"You guys ready to go?" Eddy turned to ask us. When we just stood there, mouths open like a triplet of brain-dead automatons, he added, "What's wrong?"

"You kicked—" I started.

"Tony Marchesini's ass," Sanders finished the thought.

"Good job," Candy added.

"Ah, yeah, that." He grinned, showing those buck teeth. He'd lost his glasses sometime during his assault on Tony. He found them in the dirt, wiped them clean on his bloody shirt, and stuck them back on his face. "Dad used to box. Taught me a thing or two."

"I'll fucking say." That was Willy.

"You okay, Tony?" Greg asked, as the bruised and battered teen started to sit up. Tony reached back and slugged Greg right in the nuts. Greg exhaled a sharp burst of air as he went to his knees.

"Do I..." Tony spat a clump of blood from his mouth. "... look alright, fucktard?"

"You going to apologize to her?" Eddy asked, wiping more blood off his knuckles onto his jeans.

Tony looked from Eddy to Candy, then back to Eddy. "You want me to say I'm sorry?"

"It'd be nice," Eddy said.

Tony looked back at Candy and spat one of his front teeth into the clay. "I's ssssorry," he whistled.

Chapter Six: Home

I

Summer days in Bay's End come to a dark point around seven o'clock in the evening. You can watch the sun go down behind the tree line of our little town just like watching a tea bag being dropped into water, just as fast, too. At least, that's how I remember it. Twenty years isn't pretty on the memory banks, so that's the best I can do.

The subject of my approaching birthday filled the conversation on the way home from Tony's ass whooping. Candy wondered if my parents were going to do something special for me, but I had no idea. If it was going to be a surprise, I wanted it kept that way.

"Bet your old man's gonna buy you some pussy," Eddy said, slapping his knee.

"Highly unlikely, Ed," Sanders said. "All that guy does is watch the Cubs lose, time and time again. Fudging stupid if you ask me. Now, Oakland... that's a ball team."

"Fuck the A's with a rubber hose, man," Eddy scoffed. "It's all about the Dodgers."

"Well, this is me." Sanders pointed to his house with his old Louisville Slugger. The way he looked, almost deflated, made me realize how much hanging with us had meant to him. "See you guys tomorrow?"

"Dad's got some bullshit he wants to do when he gets off work in the morning, so probably not." Eddy sighed.

"What's he do?" Sanders asked, swinging his bat over his shoulder.

"You should know; your dad hired him." Eddy grinned.

"He's the new sweep and keep? Treemont! Knew I recognized that name. Sorry, man." Sanders grimaced.

"Why you sorry?"

"For callin' him a 'sweep and keep.'"

"Ah, fuck off. It's cool, man. All's well." Eddy clapped Sanders on the shoulder.

"So what's he doing working with school out?" Candy asked.

"He's got some shit to do out at Nettles Middle School for this teacher shit coming up Saturday. Mid-school-year-hubba-bubba-bullshit. Dad says these fucking teachers gotta go to school for continuing education or some crap."

"It's like an in-service during school," Sanders informed us. "They get together and go over course studies. My dad has to go, too. Well, I gotta go."

Eddy waved him off. "Nice meeting you, buddy."

"Yeah, you, too." With that, Sanders ran across his front lawn and disappeared into his house.

"He's an all right cat, I guess," Eddy said as if he needed to speak it aloud for confirmation.

"Sanders is a sweetie." Candy grabbed my hand. "If I didn't have Trey here, I'd go for him in a heartbeat." She giggled.

I only nodded. Words weren't much for me at that moment.

"Romo's gone." I hitched my chin toward the runner.

"He's probably inside," Candy said.

I shook my head, pulling myself out of my current thoughts. "Yeah. Maybe. Whatever. Let's get out of here."

II

Mom had worked second shift at Harmony Heights two towns over in Chestnut for as long as I could remember. She'd still be working for them now if she hadn't busted her knee coming down some rain-slick steps in the parking garage a few years back. A nurse at twenty will be a nurse until she's deady, or so the saying goes, and at seventy-five, she's still my private care consultant when my shoulder gets to acting up.

The night I came home from the Marchesini beating, Dad was baking the lasagna Mom had made before going to work. He didn't talk much in those days, other than cussing at his ever-failing baseball team of choice, not since he'd been laid off from his landscaping job, and that night was no different.

"Hungry?" he asked as I walked into the kitchen to tell him I was home.

I nodded. "Sure."

He nodded back, and that was that. Dad retreated to the living room where Magnum P.I. was solving yet another case the local police should have been handling. I went to my room and popped *Sonic the Hedgehog* into my Sega Genesis and killed an hour before dinner was ready.

The silence wasn't because my father and I didn't get along. I loved the man dearly, and he loved me. It was that unspoken bond some people have. You just knew the other one cared, even when they didn't say they did. I think his parting of ways with Minnow's Man-Cured Lawns had driven him into a fit of depression he just couldn't find a way out of.

Minnow Flemming, Nathan Flemming's dad, had owned and operated Man-Cured Lawns for over thirty years, and my father had been there since the first day. It's hard to part ways with someone when you've known them for that long, but it's even rougher when it's on bad terms.

The entire situation occurred because of a bunch of bushes.

Dad swore up until the day he died ten years ago that Margie Bedford had told him, "God's honest truth," to rip those bushes separating her yard from the McDaniel's place "right the fuck out the ground." Minnow, on the other hand, never heard her say it. Minnow was weed-eating the backyard when my dad performed what Margie asked of him. He trimmed the bases down just enough to get a handsaw in there, and then cut, cut, cut, until all seven of those things were history. He was using the stump puller to remove the remnants when Margie Bedford came caterwauling out of her front door—she'd been napping as women of sixty years tended to do—screaming such a high bloody murder that Minnow heard it over the buzz of his weed eater.

When Minnow came around the side of the house, he was just in time to witness Margie Bedford's town-wide infamous breakdown. The sixty-year-old lady was rolling around in the leafy, twiggy gore of her sacred bushes, wailing like a banshee, clutching green and brown bits to her bosom like a dying child.

Minnow fired my father on the spot.

No one knows why Margie would have told Dad to rip those bushes "right the fuck out the ground" because everyone knew how much she loved them. A rumor was spread that Margie was beginning to see the back of her eyelids just around that time—she died the next year of a stroke—but Minnow wasn't hearing that. The man had a thirty-year reputation to protect and didn't need something sullying it. Even if it was his best friend and closest colleague. Dad didn't fuss or argue, but showed up in the unemployment line the very next day. He pled his case once, and that was to my mother, then he was done. If it was ever brought up, he'd reiterate the same tired old story again about how she'd told him to do it.

I can still see the regret on his face, even twenty years later and ten years after the leukemia took him. The face of a broken man. A man I see now when I look in the mirror.

The kitchen's egg timer rang, and I turned off my video game system. Dad and I sat down to plates of steaming layered pasta and ate in silence.

Chapter Seven: The White Wolf

I woke up around nine o'clock the next morning to the sound of birds outside my window. The sun had been up far longer and watched through the window as I got dressed in a Cubs jersey Dad had bought me about six months prior, though I was already starting to grow out of it. The jeans were relatively new and far from my usual holey fare. I threw on my white and red Nike's over white socks that wouldn't even be close to that color in the next hour.

I walked out of my room with one thought in my head—I couldn't hang with Eddy. He'd said he had something to do with his dad, so I was left with one of two options. Hang with Candy and Sanders, or chill around the house. The summer had been busy already, and even though I wanted to see Candy more than the world wanted to spin on an axis, I decided staying home would be the best option. Absence makes the heart grow fonder and all that.

Dad was cooking his house famous hash browns with fried eggs, and I was salivating by the time I hit the living room. The strong aromas of potatoes laced with butter and toast darkening in the oven sent my senses wild. My stomach growled as I walked into the kitchen, and Dad turned to face me when he heard it. I didn't even have to say, "Good morning, Pops."

"Smell wake you?" He flipped an egg in the pan.

"Nope." I yawned. "Just got up."

He nodded and went back to his sizzling skillets. Over the pop and crackle of the cooking breakfast, I could still hear those same birds outside, blue jays mostly. They loved the oak tree around the back of the house and had quite a few nests in the branches. They completely ignored the birdhouse Mom had set up, fully equipped with feed for them to snack on and cotton for nesting. Mom loved to wake up to their chirping. It started her day off just right, she always said. I remember wishing they would just keep singing like that forever, never ceasing, because it seemed a proper soundtrack for one to live life by.

Dad scooped up a section of hash browns the size of my head onto a plate, then laid two over easy eggs directly on top of them. He handed me the plate, smiling, and went back to the stove.

"Mom had to take an extra shift. Be home soon," he said.

"Okay." I stuffed a forkful of runny egg and fried potatoes into my waiting gullet. I was so famished that I cleared the entire plate in less than two minutes, pausing only to breathe, but mostly I did that with a mouthful, inhaling and exhaling through my nose. I ransacked that food like it was my last supper.

I took my plate to the sink, where Dad was washing dishes. "You gonna eat?"

"In a little," he said, winking.

Since Dad had been so cool that morning, having fed me a truly awesome breakfast, I looked around the kitchen for something I could do for him. I spotted the overfilled trashcan. It practically called my name.

"Gonna run the trash out to the can, okay?"

"You asking, or telling?" The smile looked good on his face. I remember thinking he should do it more often.

"Just wanted, you know, to do something nice for you."

"Go on," he said as he ran a dish-wet hand down my face. I wiped the suds from my cheek and grabbed the bag, tying it as I headed for the door.

"Trey?"

"Yeah?"

"Thanks." He winked at me, and I felt truly pleased with myself. Having a father who didn't talk much made the few words he did say rather important. I knew that even then.

Because I had been chastised for dragging a dripping bag of trash across the living room carpet a few months ago, it had been decided by unanimous decision that I was no longer to take the trash out that way. So through the back sliding glass door I went, bag of refuse in hand.

The bins were located on the side of the house next to the central heat and air box. I raised the dark blue lid and shoved the bag inside, letting the lid flop closed immediately. I had begun to turn when I heard the first growl.

That snarling beast just appeared out of thin air. First, he wasn't there, then *ta-fucking-da*, like some sick magic trick, there he was.

Romo glared at me with those off-color eyes.

I will never forget that one blue, one green gaze as long as I walk this earth.

The peach fuzz on the back of my neck stood on end, along with the fine hairs on my forearms. Static electricity shot through me, a burning sensation so intense I could feel my testicles boiling as they drew up into what felt like as far my chest. My mouth went bone-dry as the moisture beaded on my forehead and dripped into my eyes, stinging them.

I took a step back; Romo took one forward. We danced like that for what seemed an eternity while I struggled to scream, fought to make even the slightest noise that would help me flee safely.

When Romo finally shot forward, tired of our little push-me pull-you game, I finally wailed like a little girl in the midst of the Devil himself.

I started to turn, swiveling around with my right leg and pivoting with my left, when Romo caught my right calf with his teeth. I pulled hard, not knowing what else to do, and felt a sharp, piercing pain shoot up my leg into my hip. I felt pressure, a tearing, then nothing, as my leg went thankfully numb. Wrenching my calf from his mouth, still spinning into what would hopefully be my escape, I took a step forward with my damaged leg, but found it would no longer support me. Stumbling off of that leg, I managed to snap my left out in front of me.

I don't know if Romo was stunned that I'd actually broke free from his grasp, but he wasn't coming at me just then. I had my back to him, and I wasn't about to turn around and ask him the time.

Lurching forward, I managed to scream again. It wasn't really a cry for help so much as an involuntary outburst from my diaphragm; it exploded from my very soul. My thought process had ceased to exist. Many people live their entire lives not knowing what their basic survival instinct feels like. I learned just nine days shy of thirteen.

If I hadn't of screamed that second time, Dad might not have responded the way he did. Sure, he probably would have come to check on me, thinking I slammed my thumb in the trash bins lid like I had one time before, but that second scream made him grab a knife from the sink— the same one he'd used to peel potatoes with that morning—before rushing outside to check on me.

I was rounding the backside of the house when I saw Dad coming out of the doorway. I reached for him, begging him to just be suddenly within arm's length, but he wasn't. I felt the claws drag down my back as Romo struck for the second time. The weight of the monstrous canine dragged me down with him. My chin split open when I landed face first on the hard ground. Maybe if I hadn't just cut the damn grass a week and a half ago, I might have had some padding.

Teeth like razors found the nape of my neck and went to work. I felt that burning sensation again, but that time, it lasted. I felt the back of my neck come away in strips and was reminded of scotch tape being pulled from a spool. I put my hands behind my head to fight him off, but they quickly became slick with blood and utterly useless. Romo dug his lance-like claws into my back as he sought purchase.

I suddenly realized I was going to die. It was the end; I was certain. I'd never run rampant out at the Westerns again. I would never know another kiss from the lips of Candice Waters. Eddy would wonder absently why he hadn't been there to save me. Sanders would wonder who was getting my baseball card collection. Forget my first year at Bachman High, or even the thought of playing ball for the Cubbies like Dad wanted. Forget all my hopes and dreams.

My eyes closed, and my arms went limp as I waited for the end.

There was a pressure, then there wasn't. A voice, low and painful, sounding more scared than anything I had ever heard. Wet, sloppy sounds like walking through the mud, getting stuck, then getting unstuck. Singing I still can't explain. There was warmth and cold all mixed up and jumbled together. Sadness with no tears because the well had gone dry. Black with flickers of blue. A heavy feeling. My legs swinging. A bouncing, up and down... up, down. A flash of a face so tormented it would haunt my dreams for the rest of my life.

Then there was nothing.

Interlude 3: Exorcising Demons

Sorry about that, not that you noticed the delay, but I had to get rid of a few things.

The closet door now stands wide open behind me. Its contents are ablaze in the backyard, and I can see the orange glow of the fire reflected in the screen of my computer as it bleeds through my bedroom window.

In that pile of tarnished memories is a bloody Cubs jersey, a pair of jeans with a jagged hole across the outer right leg, and a pair of brown-crusted socks that were white once upon a time. I never did find those white Nikes. No one ever told me what happened to them.

Under the crackling of the fire, I can hear the dying whimpers of a ghost I have finally laid to rest. Its low growl has turned into a fading howl. It's begging to be remembered, crying to be sustained, but I will no longer let it have control over me. That fear has defined me as a man, molded me into the terrified soul I have become. No longer will it preside over my emotions. No longer will I be scared.

Eddy's frowning from his cross-legged pose on my bed. He watches me type from behind those glasses of his, the strength in his eyes replaced by worry. He knows the end is near, and as much as I want to comfort him, he knows I can't because, for the first time in my life, I need to worry about me. *If I don't vanquish these demons, if I falter on my journey, I will become just as lost as poor Eddy.*

And I can't let that happen.

Two more miles, Eddy, then I can finally let you rest.

Chapter Eight: Recovery

I

July 9ᵗʰ-23ʳᵈ, 1992

Doc Rainey said I was lucky to still have a leg. I thought it was more important that I was still among the living. Still having my head attached to my shoulders beat walking any day of the week.

It took ninety-eight stitches to patch me up. The back of my neck looked like fleshy spaghetti from what Mom told me. She laughed, but I could still see the fear in her face. They had almost lost me, and I don't think she ever forgot that.

Dad had been the worst. I tried to tell him it wasn't his fault. In the end, he had been the one who saved me. Still, he kept going on and on about how it should have been him. He should have taken out the trash or he shouldn't have cooked breakfast. In his mind, because he made that meal, because he'd been nice to me, that was why I lay recovering in a hospital. If he'd just stayed in bed and slept in, I wouldn't have felt the need to do something nice for him. Blah, blah, blah. He'd saved my life, and that was all that ever crossed my mind on the subject.

Eddy was the first of the group to come see me. His buckteeth and thick wire rims were a sight for sore eyes. Sympathy was not his thing. His shirt of the day said more about how he was taking the situation than any words could have. It was solid black with white letters across the chest that read, "BITE ME!"

"You look like shit," Eddy said. Not "How you doing?" Not "How you hanging in there?" Just a simple, obvious comment about my appearance.

He wasn't far off base, though. My right leg protruded from my gown, propped up on three flat pillows; blood had begun to pool under the white gauze, making my bandage look like a crimson Rorschach test. When Romo had gotten hold of my calf, he'd only managed to sink one fang. When I twisted and pulled, his tooth had opened the outside of my leg like a zipper. That wound had fourteen stitches on the inside, thirty on the outside. The remaining sixty-four stitches held the back of my neck together like a patchwork quilt.

"Thanks." I laughed. The catgut on the nape of my neck tugged, and my humor turned into a painful grimace.

"Saw them scoop up Romo with a shovel." Eddy chuckled. "Your old man really did a number on that dog, man. You're gonna be pulling guts from your grass for the next month."

"He deserved it." I rubbed the bandage below what used to be my hairline. They had to shave my head before putting me back together. The funny thing was, I didn't mind so much. Ironically, I was more concerned with what Candy was going to think of my new Mr. Clean impersonation.

Eddy shrugged. "Well, he won't be fucking with any more kids around the neighborhood. That's for sure."

"How's Sanders taking it?"

"His dad's all worried your pops is going to sue them."

155

"Oh, God, I doubt it. My folks are just happy I'm still around to annoy them." I was a little more careful with my laughter that time, but my stitches still stung with a burning reminder.

"People 'round town are wondering why the hell they had such a vicious mutt in the first place."

"Good question."

"They got you on any good mind fuckers?" Eddy absentmindedly played with my IV tubing.

"Nah. Just Tylenol with codeine. Makes me sleepy more than anything."

"Dad takes Oxy for his back. His doc gave him an assload before we left Toledo. He's still working on them. Likes his whiskey over his meds for pain control. He's funny when he's drinking, anyway, so we don't mind as much."

"What happened to his back?"

"Have you seen his gut? That man's walking around with a midget attached to his front. If I had a stomach like that, I'd need a fifth every day to keep the pain away, too."

We both laughed, and it felt good. I ignored the pain in my neck because I didn't want to stop. We resorted to snorting, we were laughing so hard. For the first time since I had awakened in bandages to a crying mother and a father with a bloody shirt, I felt like everything was going to be all right. Friends were better than painkillers any day of the week.

II

What should have been a two-day stay in Room 238 of Harmony Medical Center ended up being stretched into two weeks because of a medication derived from the mold that grows on cantaloupes.

Fucking penicillin.

Romo's final gift to me came on like a beast in its own right. I was fine, or so I thought, when Dr. Rainey came in after lunch on my second day in the hospital. My white count had gone through the roof because my wound was infected. Luckily, it was the wound on my leg. The nurse who'd changed the bandage on my leg the night before hadn't mentioned the pus, but Dr. Rainey sure did. To hear him tell it, I had a whole colony of bacteria building a new society in my calf.

They put me on a high dose of antibiotics. The substance looked like Pepto-Bismol, but tasted like Dubble Bubble. That flavor was a saving grace because I couldn't stand the taste of most meds. I had some Rocephin dripping into me, but the nurse told my parents that was just a starter batch. I needed the oral penicillin, too, because that's what I would be taking at home.

In three short hours, I looked as though someone had whaled on me with a cane. The welts went in sporadic patterns across my chest and arms, down my thighs, and over my butt cheeks. I looked like a pink and white leopard with chicken pox.

They nixed the penicillin, but not before the shits came on hard and fast. The amount of liquid coming out, not the frequency, caused me to end up on normal saline every four hours. I couldn't keep an ounce of solid food down, and my first three liquid diet trays ended up in the pink basin, also. Some wonderful miracle drug called Zofran cleared up the vomiting, but the fire hydrant that my backside had become went unchecked. On one of her visits, my nurse said something about letting the sickness evacuate my system. I lost ten pounds. Nothing like a good case of mud-butt to drop some weight.

Candy came in on night eight while I was making my hourly deposit in the small bathroom off of my even smaller hospital room. There I was, my boxers around my ankles, playing sprinkler with my anus, when I heard her heavenly voice.

"Trey?"

I felt my heart drop. The claustrophobic confines of the bathroom smelled like a sewer, and her visit was the last thing I needed. I tried to convince myself that if I could be quiet, she would just go away. My rectum had a different idea as it sounded like a water-filled trombone.

I heard Candy giggle and thought, *Just wonderful*, before wiping and flushing away my hopes of maintaining a decent relationship with her. Pulling up my underwear and straightening my gown, I opened the door.

"You all right?" She actually looked rather concerned.

"I must admit, I've been better." I led my IV pole out of the restroom and over to the side of the bed. I sat down and grimaced, my neck stitches pulling again.

"Mom dropped me off for the night. You don't mind, right?"

"For the night?" I asked, astonished. She was spending the night with my explosive diarrhea? I couldn't see how that could end well.

"Well, Mom couldn't find any other time to bring me, so you're stuck with me. Part of the reason it took me a week to get out here. She gets off at seven tomorrow morning. I'm yours 'til then." I missed that smile more than I missed food that wasn't in broth form.

"Pull up a seat, then." I pinched my nose with my thumb and index finger. "It won't smell pretty. Just warning you."

"Oh, whatever. Did I ever tell you my granddad had a colostomy bag?" she asked as she sat in the reclining chair by the window.

"What the hell is that?"

"It's a bag that connects to a hole in your stomach so you can poop through it."

"What the hell?" I drew my head back as if she'd just suddenly thrown something at me. The back of my neck screamed, and I bleated like a sheep.

"He had colon cancer, and they had to remove it. Fat lot of good that did. He died three months later. But before he died, Mom and me used to have to help him change it. I will never forget that shit. Literally." She frowned, crinkling her nose as though she could still smell her granddad's lingering odor.

"I'm sorry. That sucks."

"Ah, it's okay. I guess it wasn't so bad. I did get to spend more time with him before he died. Whether it was changing a shitty bag or not, guess it didn't matter." Her face changed to one of remembrance, and she offered me a wan smile. "Last time I was in this hospital was the night he died."

I remained silent, not knowing what to say even if I could have spoken. I only listened. In the end, I suppose that's all she needed me to do.

"He was a good guy. He'd buy me flowers on my birthday and take me out to Rifle Park to swing before I got too old for it." She swallowed, and I watched the lump slide down her throat. "Before he retired, he used to work out in the Westerns. He was a machine operator on the grinder. He'd tell me stories about how times were good back then. People helped other people and didn't complain about the long hours and crappy pay." She shrugged as if to make her point.

"Granddad told me my mom wasn't much different than me when she was growing up. Her eyes were just as old as mine, or something like that. Like we'd seen too much before our time. Mom was a funny little girl to hear him tell it. I don't know where her sense of humor went. Maybe Dad got it in the separation." I felt like laughing, but I didn't. "Granddad never did like my father. Even I could see that. I guess he was right, huh?"

Not wanting her to stop talking just because I opened my mouth, I just shrugged.

"Yeah, he was right. Dad used to tell me that my mother was a pain in the ass, said she wasn't good for anything. Mom never once said anything bad about him, not even when she filed the papers. I had to find out from a friend of mine that my dad was fooling around. That's some bullcrap, ain't it?" I nodded. "I mean, I wondered back then, maybe we just weren't good enough for him. Maybe I could have done something. Been less of an annoyance, right? Been a better daughter? Maybe that would have kept him home." She wiped a renegade tear and exhaled sharply. "Forget it."

"No," I said. "Go on."

"It's just that, Mom's so pretty and so nice. She never deserved what Dad put her through. She didn't talk to me for almost a week after she found out about his affair. I had no clue back then. I thought I had done something wrong, that I had been bad or something. Turned out it was just good ol' Dad the Jerk, and it didn't have anything to do with me." Candy was crying. No restraint, just free-flowing tears. "I hated him for that. Hated him for making me think there was something wrong with me."

"There's nothing wrong with you," I said. "You're... perfect."

Her eyes met mine, and she smiled through her tears. I'd never seen that look before. She got up from the recliner and came to the side of my bed. Everything went in slow motion, like movement under water. Candy pushed the IV pole out of the way and leaned in over my railing. A cool hand played over my cheek as her thumb trailed down the bridge of my nose. Candy leaned in and kissed me. Her warm lips enveloped mine, and I melted under their heat. The kiss felt like the first, startling and new. Her hand slithered around the back of my neck and pulled me closer. I gasped as her fingers found my bandage, and she jerked away.

"I'm sorry," she said, worry in her eyes.

"Fuck that," I whispered. I latched a hand behind her head and pulled her back. Our mouths connected in electric waves, and I could sense every hair on my body stand on end. My groin tingled as I stiffened. I could feel myself growing, popping out of the hole in my boxers and raising my gown just enough to be noticeable.

A warm hand that was definitely not my own found my length and squeezed.

"Whoa," I moaned into her mouth, my eyes popping open.

"Shhh," she whispered against my lips.

Movement below stole my breath. I'd only ever felt my own hand there. A random thought ran through my mind—*How does she know what she's doing down there?*—but didn't stay long as my body tightened and my soul seemed to rush from my very being.

III

Dad came in the next morning. He found Candy snoring in the recliner by the window. I was already awake and watching Saturday morning cartoons. He walked up to the side of the bed, a clear plastic trash bag in his hands.

"Hey," he said as he laid the bag on the nightstand.

"Hey, Dad." I turned off the TV to give him my full attention. "What's that?" I jerked my chin at the bag, and my stitches caught. I never learned, like a mouse that constantly snips at the electrified cheese in his cage.

"Your clothes."

"I'm going home!" The thought of home-cooked meals, the sun on my face, and a Genesis controller in my hands made me happier than I could express.

"Not so much." He frowned. "It's the clothes from your... accident." He hung his head lower, and I saw him break. I didn't ask why he'd brought them or how he'd come to have them. The look of memories running across his face was enough to make an auctioneer speechless.

I reached out and grabbed his wrist. He met my eyes and fought to smile. He lost that battle horribly.

"She stayed the night?" Dad jerked his chin in Candy's direction.

I nodded. "Yeah. Her Mom should be here soon." I explained how it was the only way she would have been able to come, and he told me he understood.

"You all right?" he asked in a hushed voice. Looking back, I'm sure just the sight of me laid up like I was had him on the verge of tears.

"If I could stop moving my head, I'd be fine." I admitted.

"You, uh..." He fought for the words, and I could see the torment in his eyes. "... sleeping okay?"

I should've lied, but I told him the truth.

The house is dark. I'm running down an endless hallway, fighting to gain ground, struggling to maintain a good distance between me and the snarling beast at my heels. Romo is impossibly large, larger than everything. I don't know how I know this because I haven't seen him. I just know, and knowing has scared me to death. All I can do is run. Run until everything on me burns and I can't breathe and I can't stop and there's no end to this damn hallway. There's hot breath on my neck. Spittle showers the back of my forearms from the monstrous dog's hideous mouth. I'm running and running and running, until it lunges, attacks. And then I wake up.

"I'm sorry," Dad said when I finished my story. "God..." The tears came. "I'm so damn sorry, Trey."

"It's okay, Dad." I started crying, too. "You saved me," I told him for the umpteenth time. "I wouldn't be here if it wasn't for you."

"When you were three, you stopped breathing."

That hit me like a slap to the face. I'd never heard that. He had my full attention. I couldn't have pulled myself away if I wanted.

"Your mother came home one night after work and found you in your bed, blue. I was asleep on the couch. I'd been waiting on her to come home and... and I just fell asleep. Thank God she's a nurse." He stopped, gathered his strength, then continued, "She started reviving you, fighting to save you while I snored in the living room." I could see the anger on his face. Anger directed at himself. Pent up, self-despising, self-deprecating anger. I'd never forget that face. It scared the hell out of me.

"She was doing chest compressions when that little blue chewed-up piece of gum popped out of your mouth." I had a flash of my bedroom then: brown carpet with one tiny hard patch in it. It had grown black over the years, but you could still see bits where the blue peeked through the dirt. "You came out of it all right, but your mother didn't. She hated me for months after that. Night after night, I'd find her asleep in your bed. I never once apologized. Not because I didn't want to, but because I had no right to say it. Sorry wasn't good enough."

"Dad." I squeezed his wrist. "You couldn't have—"

"I gave you the gum." It was final. As though he were telling me I couldn't have dinner because I hadn't cleaned my room. That way parents say things, and you know that's the end of the conversation.

He stood there for another moment before turning and leaving.

I wondered for years if my father ever forgave himself for the blue gum or for Romo. Neither had been his fault. Mom never left him because she realized that at some point, too. Sure, he'd screwed up, but he was only human. Just like with Romo and me, Dad had been dealt a poor hand. It wasn't the last time he spilled his guts to me, but it was the first.

My father, the heavy heart.

IV

On my last night in the hospital, I awoke with a start, my eyelids fluttering and my breath gone. The nape of my neck made itself known, but I was more interested in the blaring music and the strobe-light effect of the TV as MC Hammer glided across the screen. Looking left and right, ignoring the burning under the dressing on the back of my neck, I hunted for an explanation.

I found him sitting in the recliner by the window, smiling.

"What, Franklin? Don'tcha like the tunes?" Officer Mack asked as he nodded to the beat of *U Can't Touch This*. "Not too fond of this nigger, but you know." He shrugged and rose from the chair. "Beats the hell outta country lost-my-wife-and-dog-to-the-postman bullshit. Pardon my French, o' course."

I didn't know why he was there, and I wasn't about to ask. Fear had stolen everything but concern for my own well-being. Keeping quiet was the best course of action when dealing with Mack.

"Dog did a number on you, Franklin." Mack approached the side of my bed shaking his head. "I was almost certain it was the end of our little... friendship. That would just be too bad now, wouldn't it?"

He was dressed in his blues with his patrolman's cap tucked under his right arm. As he came to the side of my bed, he placed the hat on his head and cocked it to the side. He smiled at me from under there, shadows and light from the TV fighting for purchase on his grinning mug. His scar twitched.

"Your dad cut that mutt up real good. The thought occurred to me to haul him in for animal cruelty, but I decided that would be a little much." He winked.

I wanted my mommy.

Mack was rolling something around his hand that I couldn't see in the dark. But I could see his fingers working on something. I didn't think I wanted to know. Mainly because, somewhere in the back of my mind, I knew exactly what was there.

"You got off easy, Franklin. That dog really coulda fucked you up something serious. Fucked your shit right up. Pardon my French, o' course." Officer Mack reached for the remote on my lap and turned off the TV. Those few seconds in complete darkness before my eyes adjusted, with Officer Mack hovering over me, were some of the most terrifying seconds of my life. I heard him wheezing, breathing raggedly, and the smell of cherry cough drops hung in the air. His large hand rested in my lap.

"I'd hate to think of a world without you, Trey," he whispered. "Just what would I do without you kids fucking with me all the time?"

Pardon your French, I thought.

He gave my leg a little pat. "I shudder to think we just wouldn't see each other again."

My mouth went dry, and my heart threatened to burst out of my chest as I realized his hand was gone from my lap. I followed the *clop, clop, clop* of his footsteps as he made his way to the door. Light flooded my hospital room as the door was jerked open.

"Tell Eddy Treemont I said, 'What's up,'" Mack said as he pulled the door closed behind him.

I struggled to find the light in the dark. The brightness that had come in from the hallway had caused my eyes to readjust, and I was blind for a good minute before I found the call light. I pressed every single button on that fucking thing before my light flickered on.

I sat there, my breathing coming in hot spurts, my heart in my throat. Then, I saw what Mack had left on my lap.

Lying next to the remote was a single burnt husk of a cherry bomb. A dark circle formed around it like a frame as I pissed my bed for the first time since I was five.

~ * * * ~

I was able to flush what was left of that cherry bomb down the toilet before my nurse came. I acted embarrassed when I told her I had wet the bed, but she assured me it was all right.

Giving her the "I had a nightmare about the dog" line sealed the deal. She brought some warm water in a basin and left me alone while I cleaned up. I called her back when I was done, and she had the nurse's assistant come in to change my bed.

I remember dreaming again that night, but not of Romo. Officer Mack had me strapped to a chair while he force-fed me several spoonfuls of fireworks. Fully lit ones.

The next day was my birthday. Honestly, I don't remember a minute of it.

Chapter Nine: Homecoming

I

July 24ᵗʰ, 1992

Two weeks and one day later, I was finally allowed to go home. I carried with me memories of my first hand job, a reflective father, an unsettling revelation, and a severe penicillin allergy. Technically, I was discharged at five that afternoon, but I had to wait around until Mom got off at eleven before I caught the wheelchair express down to the lobby. Mom left the car idling in the turnabout and came around to help. She called the nurse Nancy and thanked her for bringing me down to the car. Nancy winked at me. Waving, she disappeared back through the hospital doors. She was a nice enough lady, but I silently prayed I never had to see her again.

The stitches on the back of my neck had started to itch something fierce. Every so often on the way home, I would reach back, my fingers set to claw, and Mom would slap my hand away before I did anything stupid. She'd smile. I'd frown. Back and forth we went for twenty miles before Highway 607 turned into Main Street, and we arrived in Bay's End. It was fifteen minutes until midnight when our headlights found Hibiscus. So many cars were in front of our house that some had to park across the street in front of Eddy's place.

I smiled, knowing they were all there because of me—my own little homecoming party. Several different feelings came over me, but the most prevalent was a sense of calm happiness.

Mom swung the wagon into the driveway behind Sulan Sanderson's BMW. Sanders was sitting on the trunk of his father's car with Candy beside him. They both bounced in the glow of Mom's car headlights. Candy had a smile etched on her face, and her black hair was pulled up tight in a ponytail that bobbed as she waved.

Pushing open my car door before Mom had even put the car in *Park*, I heard Metallica's *Enter Sandman* coming from the house. Raised voices mixed with the tune, making it sound like a concert.

"What's up, dude?" I asked Sanders as I hobbled up beside the BMW.

"Party time, Trey!" Sanders threw back his head and trilled like a Mariachi.

"How you doing?" Candy asked.

"Much better now," I told her, not having to add that it was because she was there.

"Hello, kids," Mom said as she passed. "You coming inside?"

Sanders grinned. "Of course."

"My mom said she wanted to talk to you when you got back. She's off tonight. I think she has your order," Candy said.

"Sounds good. See you inside." Mom walked up the porch steps and into the house.

"You look good enough to eat. Wait. Something already tried that." Sanders laughed.

I flipped him off. That gesture reminded me to ask, "Where's Eddy?"

"Inside. His dad's telling drunk stories, and Eddy's making darn sure he doesn't completely tarnish their family name." Sanders pointed to the house where I could see Mr. Treemont's belly jiggling in the window. "Dude's been drinking since he got here."

"From what Eddy says, he's funnier when he drinks." I reached for the back of my neck but caught myself before I started scratching. I just imagined Mom slapping my hand away, and that helped rectify the action. Sighing, I stuck both of my hands deep inside the pockets of my jeans.

"Something like that." Sanders laughed. "The big guy *has* laughed hardest at his own jokes. But I wouldn't say he's funnier."

"Just louder," Candy added.

"Time to go, I suppose." Sanders slid off the back of the luxury coupe and landed with a *slap* on the driveway. He bowed and extended his hand to Candy. "Can I help muh'lady down?"

She slapped his wrist playfully. "My knight in shining armor. Wow, your head *is* really shiny, Trey. You can help your lady down. Right?"

"No prob, Bob." I placed a hand under each of her arms and braced her while she floated off the edge of the trunk. My thumbs pressed into the soft mounds of her breasts, and I hoped she didn't notice. Once she was on her feet, she adjusted her bra and glared at me. I felt my cheeks grow warm.

"Copping a feel, sire?"

"What can I say?" I shrugged. "I didn't see a 'hands off the merchandise' sign. So I put hands on."

"Cute."

"Okay then," Sanders said. "I'll see you two inside."

"Later," Candy and I said in unison.

Once Sanders walked inside, Candy met my eyes. "So, what did you want to talk to me about?"

The morning after my unwanted meeting with Mack, I'd called Candy and told her we needed to talk. Steadying myself for the bad news ahead, I recounted the events that had left me with a lap full of piss and a spent firework.

"No shit?" Shock stole over her face. "How could he have known? He didn't see us. Did he?"

"I don't know, but I don't like it. That bastard is far from stable." Forgetting about my bald scalp, I reached up to run my fingers through my hair, and my hand came back slick with sweat. The night was rather cool, so I attributed the perspiration to nerves.

"What are we gonna do?"

"Beats the hell outta me, Candy." I shrugged. "This just keeps getting deeper."

"Yeah." She focused on the ground at her feet. Her face bore an expression I couldn't pinpoint. A sadness, yet darker.

"What's wrong?" I asked.

"Ah, nothing." Candy kicked at a stray weed poking out of a crack in the cement drive. Her mind was suddenly somewhere else, distracted.

"Come on." I put my arm around her shoulders. "If you can't tell me..."

"It's nothing. Really," she said with a meek smile that I instantly knew was fake.

"Problems?" I pushed.

"Trey?"

"Yeah?"

"Drop it," she said sternly.

"Fine, then. But we gotta do something about Maniac Mack before he gets some harebrained idea in his head to haul us in for bombing him." I released her shoulders and leaned against the trunk of the BMW. "Almost becoming dog food for a demonic canine kinda sets your priorities in line."

"Why are you joking about that? You coulda died, jerk." Candy shot me a glare that made my heart hurt. "I coulda lost you, like I lost my granddad."

"Sorry." I frowned. "I figure it's either laugh or cry, and I think every bit of moisture in my body was drained after Penicillin's Revenge."

She finally smiled. "Hush."

"Seriously." I sucked in my cheeks. "I about washed away in a flood of diluted brownie mix!"

"Yuck, Trey!" She slapped me. "That's gross."

"At least you're smiling." I put the palm of my hand against her cheek and leaned in to kiss her.

I was taken aback when she pulled away. "What's wrong?"

She exhaled sharply. "Nothing."

"I call bullshit."

"You know Mr. Lance?" The question hung on the air for a minute while I placed the name. I knew it, but the face eluded me. Ryan and Jamie from down the street popped into my mind. Mr. Lance was their father. "Oh, yeah, right. What about him?"

"Him and Mom have been... you know." She made an O with her thumb and forefinger and slid the index finger of her other hand in and out of it.

"Your mom's *doing* Mr. Lance?" I was astonished. His wife had just died a couple

185

months ago. I didn't think he even left the house anymore. I sure hadn't seen neither hide nor hair of the twins since their mother had passed. Then, I find out that he'd been laying it to Carrie Waters, who was freshly out of a relationship herself.

"I can't say much about it." Her eyes became hollow. It was like she was fading from me, reliving something she didn't want to. "He seems to like *me* well enough."

"Whataya mean?"

"Never mind." And that was that. I knew she wasn't going into any more details, so I left it alone.

Then she asked, "What are we gonna do about Officer Mack?"

"Stay far the fuck away from him is what I want to do." I noticed my shoe was untied. I bent over to tie it, and my stitches pulled. "Fuck!" I growled as I rubbed my bandage.

"You okay?" Candy grimaced. "Sorry. Stupid question."

"It's all right." I laced up my sneaker and tied it in a double bow. I stood back up just in time to see the cruiser come around the corner of Lime and onto Hibiscus. "Speak of the devil."

Candy turned to look his way. "What the hell does he want?"

"Checking on us, I guess."

Officer Mack slowed down in front of my place, but didn't stop. In the glow of the streetlights, I saw him waving as he glided down the street. He hit the end of the road and made a left, disappearing out of sight.

"Why doesn't he just make a move? He can't be scared of us." Candy rubbed her forearms. I could see the chill bumps there, defined in shadows on her bare skin.

"What the fucking hell are you two doing out here all by your lonesome?" Eddy came around the front of the BMW clapping his hands as he spoke.

Candy and I both jumped.

"Dude! Really?" I said, my breathing coming fast.

"Jackass," Candy groaned. She straightened her t-shirt as if it was crooked.

"Officer Mack got you all pissing your pants or something?" Eddy grinned with his buckteeth. His lips were orange in the sodium vapor of the streetlights.

"You saw him?" I asked.

"Couldn't help it. That's why I came out. Creepy motherfucker acting all stalker-ish and shit." Eddy leaned forward, checking the end of the block for Officer Mack. He didn't say that's what he was doing, and he didn't have to. As big and brave as Eddy Treemont was, Officer Mack scared him. There was no mistaking that on Eddy's face.

"He knows, Eddy," I said.

"Yeah, I know that." Eddy rummaged in his back pocket. He pulled out a closed fist and laid something on the trunk. Another burned-up cherry bomb.

"Fucking hell." I sighed. "That's really not good."

"Found it in my mailbox last Tuesday," Eddy said. "I was going outside to grab the mail, and I seen him pulling away from the house. I checked the box, and I'll be damned if it wasn't there." Eddy pushed his wire rims up his nose. "Fucker gives me the willies."

"Yeah, me, too." Candy shivered.

"He paid me a little visit while I was at Harmony. Gave me one of those before he walked out." I pointed at the used up cherry bomb. "I flushed the thing. No way was I keeping it."

"Probably the same day he left one for me," Eddy remarked.

"Probably." I nodded. "You get one?" I asked Candy.

She laughed nervously. "Not yet."

"*Yet* being the operative word there." Eddy picked up the cherry bomb and placed it in his front pocket. "You know what I think?"

"Enlighten us, Madame Zorka." The lady in question used to run a psychic shack out on I-29 just inside Bay's End city limits. That was years before Eddy moved into town, so he just looked confused.

"Please do," Candy added.

"I think he's waiting on something."

"Waiting," I whispered, flashing to Hap Carringer's retirement party—Mack sitting on the stage, not really watching... but waiting.

"Like waiting for one of us to fuck up and do something retarded. Then, he'll just bring down the hammer and be done with us. Right now, all he has is criminal mischief, and that don't hold water in court. Not at our age. Trust me. I should know."

And we did trust him. I never did ask how Eddy knew so much about juvenile court and its bylaws, but I was sure he was well informed. I

189

had only known him for four weeks, but I was certain he'd not been an angel before coming to The End. Hell, it had been his idea to use the cherry bombs. Still, we were in it together, and if one of us went down, the other two would follow right along. No questions asked.

Inside my house, Bob Marley sang, *I Shot the Sheriff* at an ungodly volume.

II

"I fear so sorry. Reary, Trey." Sulan Sanderson was the first one to come over to me when the three of us finally went inside. His eyes were puffy, and he smelled of alcohol. I didn't recall Sanders ever telling me his dad drank, but considering he was feeling responsible for my attack, I could allow him a couple hard ones. "Can I e'er repay you?"

"It's all right, Mr. Sanderson." I gave him a small smile as I pushed past him and out of the foyer.

The air was thick with body heat and the cloying scent of cigar smoke. Mr. Treemont was conversing loudly with Minnow and my dad over by the window. A large stogy jutted from the corner of his mouth, thick gray clouds billowed from the tip. That didn't surprise me. What did shock me was the fact that my father had a cigar tucked between his index and middle finger along with a glass of translucent brown liquid. Minnow laughed at something my father said and topped off each man's glass before they had a chance to empty it.

Mom was entertaining a group of women in the kitchen. I could hear their raised voices and laughter over the sound of Billy Idol singing *White Wedding* on the stereo system. I ignored them as I moseyed over to find out why Minnow was there.

"Hey, Dad," I said as I came up beside him. He smiled down at me, and I watched the glassiness of his eyes fade for a brief second.

"S'here he ish," Dad slurred, clapping me on the back. I winced, glad he hadn't slapped my neck. "Dash muh boy, Minna! Ta'es a lickin' and keeps on kickin'."

"You's a tough one, kid." Minnow toasted the air in front of me with his glass.

"My Eddy woulda boxed that dog's ears. Fucking mutt woulda cut himself up after my boy

192

gotta hold of him," Mr. Treemont bellowed, his inebriated laughter *Boomed!* "Not that yer boy ain't somethin', Franklin. Just... you know." Mr. Treemont winked at my father, and all three men laughed.

"Your dad's coming back to work for me, Trey. Whaddaya say about that?" Minnow asked with a grin.

"Really?" That was the best news I could have gotten that day. Officer Mack faded from my memory, if only for just a moment. Smiling, I wrapped an arm around Dad's waist and squeezed.

"Yep," Minnow said over the top of his glass before taking a drink. He swallowed hard, the way only drunks do, and met my beaming eyes. "Figured times are rough enough and all. Man needs to be able to support his family."

I looked up into my father's bloodshot eyes. "That's really awesome, Dad! I'm happy for you."

"Ands I'm shappy fer you, Shlugger." Dad ruffled my hair. "Shit. Ish hot in here." He tugged at the front of his shirt. "Dis boy gonna play for the Cubbies, jesh you wait!"

I started to move away. "I'll talk to you guys later."

"Good ta hash you back," Dad slurred. I just waved him away, figuring to let him celebrate. He deserved it.

Candy and Eddy were sitting on the couch. I sat down on the coffee table and leaned back on my palms. Eddy was reading a copy of *Good Housekeeping* my mother always kept around for company. The issue was three years old, and I was sure Eddy was just trying to keep himself occupied.

"What do you guys wanna do?" I asked over the music.

"It's your homecoming party, shithead. You tell us," Eddy said from behind the magazine's glossy cover.

"I'm just waiting on Mom to pull us home." Candy glanced toward the kitchen where I could see her mother talking to mine, Mrs. Treemont, and Jenna Wales. "We normally don't stay long at parties."

"I don't know." I shrugged. "Mom has a way of keeping people busy. I'm sure the night's just started."

"It's already past midnight. What else could be going on?" Eddy snapped the periodical as though it were a newspaper and crossed his legs like some executive going over business at a luncheon.

"You never know when it comes to my mother." I sniffed and found something new lingering in the air. "Somebody grilling?"

Candy automatically dropped her head again, and Eddy answered, "That retarded kid's old man is cooking."

"Jamie's dad?" I asked. Though Ryan and Jamie were twins, Jamie had been born with Down Syndrome. Talk about a shitty hand. Poor Jamie had a perfectly normal sibling, a straight-A student, a leader of the pack kind of cat, and he was born... well, bad luck didn't get much worse. "Where are they? Out back?"

"Uh, yeah," Eddy scoffed. "Where do you think they're barbecuing? Your fucking bathroom?"

"Hush." Candy slugged him in the chest. "You're such a jerk sometimes. Jesus!"

"Hey!" Eddy wailed, rubbing his pecs. "I was just stating the obvious." He turned to me as he threw down the *Good Housekeeping*. "You know I was just joking. Right, man?"

"Sure." I shrugged. "She's just a little... overprotective."

"Fine. I'll just let everyone walk all over my guy and smile. Nothing to see here. Nothing at all. Just some kid getting picked on. Same shit, different day!"

"Whatever." I flipped my wrist at her, waving her off. "I'm going to go see Ryan and Jamie. You guys coming?" I got up and pulled my underwear from my crack. My old boxers were starting to get on my nerves. Hopefully, Mom and I would go clothes shopping before school started, or my boxers would end up fitting like briefs.

"S'pose so," Eddy said as he rose from the couch. He yawned, stretching hard, and I noticed his tongue was green.

"What the hell have you been eating?" I asked.

"Your momma."

"Last time you had some pussy, pussy had you," Candy rejoined. That was one of the more disgusting things I had ever heard her say, but I laughed nonetheless. Something was different about her. It wasn't just the boobs, the clothes, or the fact that she'd stroked me off in my hospital bed. Something about her was older, but it felt wrong.

Eddy gave her an O face and slapped his cheeks. We made our way through the gaggle of geese gossiping in the kitchen.

"Hey, Trey." Jenna Wales waved and smiled as I passed. "Good to see you home."

She was much taller than I remembered, and skinnier. The last time I had seen her was at Hap Carringer's retirement party. Back then, she'd been a little bigger in the hips. Probably just baby fat. She was one sexy sight for my thirteen-year-old eyes. Her golden hair hung straight down her back in a ponytail, a pink scrunchie keeping everything together. Her painted-on jeans hugged her ass, making it look like an apple. And her bra... well, it was a miracle the way it pushed her tits up to her chin under the low V of her yellow sweater. That was the first time I had seen her out of uniform in at least four years. I struggled to remember how old she was and settled on twenty-two.

Back when Mom used to babysit her, Mom would take pictures and pretend Jenna was a model. Mom still had some of those pictures lying around the house, and I had seen them on occasion. Jenna had been a porker. The years after had been kind enough, and she'd developed into the raging beauty I saw before me now. I wasn't too surprised she had joined the police force, but I was shocked to find out she'd been stuck behind a desk in dispatch. I could see her running the streets, fighting crime. Answering phones just seemed far too boring for her. She looked the part of an adventurer, not an operator.

"Thanks." I grinned as her blue eyes met mine. I could lie and say I didn't get that tingling feeling downstairs, but that would be a load of crap.

Candy must've noticed my infatuation because she grabbed my hand and led me out the back door. I about snapped my neck trying to look back at Jenna.

Damn, but she had a great ass.

III

The smell of the grill flooded my senses as soon as we stepped out onto the concrete slab that was my back porch. Aromas of sizzling meat and steaming corn drove my stomach nuts. I grinned from ear to ear as I took in everything.

Mr. Lance stood behind the open gas grill with his hands on his hips. He glared down into the rising smoke, assessing his work, frowning as if something just didn't look quite right. He reached down to the table beside the grill and picked up a pair of tongs. He rearranged the hamburgers, hot dogs, and foil-wrapped cobs before finally catching the three of us watching him from the back step.

"Hey, kids." He waved us over. "Come to see what's cooking?"

Corporal Jude Lance had come home from Iraq a changed man. Before Desert Storm, Mr. Lance was the cock of the walk around The End. He'd scored the prettiest girl that side of Chestnut, a saucy little minx named Willa Monroe. Their love affair had been quick, and the twins came shortly after they met. He had been sent off to Kuwait during the first skirmishes and spent nine months in Baghdad. When Willa had swallowed the business end of his Walther PPK, Jude Lance had been allowed to go home to tend to his preteen boys.

Their story was a real-life tragedy. Ryan came out first. At almost ten pounds, he was a big baby. Ryan was a natural birth, but they had to cut Jamie out of Willa. Jamie weighed in at just under thirteen pounds, and he had Down Syndrome. Everyone assumed that Jamie's constant needs had made Willa kill herself.

Jude Lance was a short man, almost childlike, with a doughy face and red cheeks. If the man had a white beard, instead of the black one he'd grown after Willa's death, he might have looked like Santa Claus's younger brother. My father told me once that it was the small guys you had to watch out for: "They have piss and vinegar running through their veins," I remember him saying. Boy, he couldn't have been more right about that one as I would come to find out.

"How long before everything's ready?" Eddy coughed as he waved a rogue cloud of smoke away from his face.

"Few more minutes." Mr. Lance smiled, looking Eddy up and down. "And who are you, pumpkin?"

Pumpkin? Needless to say, I found the term odd.

"His name is Eddy Treemont." I looked at Candy to see if she found "pumpkin" as strange as I did, but she just stared at her feet, kicking at a blade of grass that had grown up through a crack in the concrete. Her hands were shoved in the pockets of her jeans, and her wrists were white from lack of blood.

Mr. Lance must've noticed her also. "What's wrong, Candy?"

Candy? As far as I knew, I was the only one who called her that.

"Huh?" She snapped her head up to look at him. The action caused my own neck to hurt and made me rub at my bandage. "Oh, nothing." She shook her head.

Mr. Lance looked back at Eddy. "Treemont? Well, that's not a name I've heard often."

"It is what it is." Eddy shrugged. "Had it my whole life."

"I would hope so." Mr. Lance aimed the tongs at Eddy and winked. "You guys just moved in a little less than a month ago, right?" he asked as he flipped a burger on the grill. The fire popped and sizzled, flaring a little where grease oozed down off the patty.

"Yep," Eddy said.

"Trey!" Jamie came blundering around the side of the house, skipping like mad. "Trey-day!"

"Hey, Jamie!" I yelled. It had been months since I'd seen him or his brother. I wasn't too shocked to see Ryan following him, walking instead of skipping.

Jamie had the telltale signs of Down's Syndrome all over his face, the too-large forehead, big lips, drool constantly present on his lower lip, and the massive lolling tongue that just wouldn't stay in his mouth. He wore a Superman T-shirt that night and a pair of acid-washed jeans that were far too big for him. He had both thumbs hitched into the belt loops to help keep his pants up.

Ryan looked like hell washed over. He was thin, emaciated even, and his brown, ear-length hair was greasy. It clung to his forehead in wiry strands. His white wife-beater shirt was stained with red blotches that looked like they might have come from Kool-Aid. He wore a pair of cargo shorts that hung down below his knees. His chicken legs protruded from the holes like two sticks.

Jamie crashed into me like a thundering, stampeding elephant. His sloppy mouth wet the front of my shirt, but I didn't complain. It was just one of those things you got used to when you hung out with him. Jamie squeezed me until I was sure my brains would pop out the top of my head like toothpaste when the tube is rolled. Just when I couldn't take much more, he released me, and my pent-up breath exploded from me in a burst of laughter.

"Good to see you, too, Jamie," I stammered.

"You dotta see my bubberflies, Trey-day. Dotta see my bubberflies. Come on!" Jamie snatched my hand and began to drag me across the backyard.

"Not right now, Jamie," Mr. Lance said. I noticed Eddy and Candy were killing themselves laughing. "Gotta eat real soon, Jay," Mr. Lance added.

"Don't dotta eat," Jamie roared, slapping his free hand on his thigh. "Dotta show Trey-day my bubberflies! Not seen 'em. He not seen 'em!"

"Calm down, buddy," Mr. Lance cooed. "He can come see them tomorrow."

"Dotta go, go, go, now, Daddy," Jamie whimpered.

"Jay," Ryan's voice cracked. "Dad said no."

"Bubberflies?" Jamie whined, looking to me for help. "You wanna see my bubberflies, right, Trey-day?"

"Sure thing, Jamie." I pointed to my leg. "But I got a boo boo, and I can't go right now."

"Oh, yeah! Da doogie got your leg and went *Rawrrr!* My daddy told me 'bout dat." Jamie's spittle splashed across my face, and I wiped it away, trying not to look too disgusted.

"Yes, the bad dog bit Trey and then went to heaven," Eddy said.

Candy kicked his leg. "Stop it."

"What?" Eddy groaned, oblivious.

"Never mind." Candy sighed. "He really does have a wicked butterfly collection, Trey."

"Sweet," I exclaimed. "I'll definitely come down and see it this week. Okay?"

I could see the disappointment in Jamie's face, but I also noticed the excitement in Ryan's.

"You gonna come by for real?" Ryan asked. He wasn't as visually excited as Jamie, but I could see a faint hope in his eyes. I felt bad for him, wondering how long it'd been since they'd had friends over.

I shrugged. "Sure, why not?"

"Dad just says—"

"Who's ready to eat?" Mr. Lance yelled much too loudly. I turned and found him giving Ryan a strange look. Ryan hung his head. I didn't hear another word from him the rest of the night.

IV

Everyone finally started leaving at two o'clock in the morning. The food was devoured, all the liquor Mr. Treemont had brought was gone, and my father was passed out cold in his recliner. Jenna stayed to help Mom with the cleanup while Candy, Eddy, and I sat on the front porch watching everyone else leave.

Minnow was the first to leave, since he had to work the next morning. I had no idea when Dad was starting back with him. I only hoped it wasn't immediately because Dad was going to have one hell of a hangover. Candy's mom let her hang around for a little while longer, but went home when everyone else left. Eddy's parents were some of the last to go, since all they had to do was walk across the street.

"That was fun," Eddy scoffed. He'd been bored all night. If there wasn't a fight or an adventure, Eddy wasn't satisfied.

"I don't know. I had fun." I wrapped my hand around Candy's, and she laid her head on my shoulder.

"Everyone was just glad to have you back, is all," Candy said.

"Would you two get a fucking room? God, it feels like I'm hanging out with a couple birds during mating season." Eddy knuckled his chin and placed his elbow on his knee.

"Get over yourself," I told him.

"He's just jealous, I think." Candy yawned, stretching against me.

"Fuck being jealous. I get all the girls!" Eddy flexed his arm and kissed his bicep.

"Yeah, right." Candy giggled.

"So," Eddy said, "what are we gonna do tomorrow? Little more than a month 'til school starts. Romo ruined half our fucking summer."

"Our summer? What about Trey's summer? I think he got the worst end of it." Candy lifted her head off my shoulder as she spoke. "We just had to deal with him not being around. Our illustrious leader." She kissed me on the cheek, and it felt good, warm.

"I did just fine without him." Eddy shined those buck teeth our way.

"Yeah? And that's why you were over my house everyday asking me to do something with you?" Candy came back.

"Just thought you were fucking lonely. Sorry for being sympathetic to your plight, bitch." Eddy flipped her off.

"Eat me." Candy stuck out her tongue, raspberrying the air between us.

"Gladly! But I think Trey might disapprove of me munching your fish taco."

I'd had enough. "Guys, quit it."

Candy sighed. "He started it."

"And I'll end it." Eddy stuck his own tongue out at her.

"Anyway," I interjected. "I promised Ryan and Jamie I'd come over this week. I guess we could go hang out with them tomorrow. Whataya say?"

Eddy cringed. "That Jamie fucker gonna drool on me?"

"Stop with that shit. He's a good kid. It's not his fault he's different," Candy barked.

"Sorry. Shit. I didn't mean anything by it. I think I'll hang at home. That Ryan dude fucking reeks." Eddy pinched his nose.

"He didn't used to be like that," I told him. "I think it has something to do with his mom shooting herself."

"Amongst other things," Candy whispered.

Before I could ask what she meant, Eddy mouthed off again. "She blew her brains out? Damn. That's fucked up."

"Really did a number on all of them." I shook my head, remembering the day they found her. "It was about four in the afternoon, and we were walking home. I left Candy at her door and watched Ryan and Jamie go inside. I was halfway home when Ryan came out of the house, screaming about blood and shit."

"He fucking *found* her?" Eddy asked, his mouth hanging open in shock. "That's rough, man!"

"He stepped into what was left of her head," Candy added.

"Yuck!" Eddy gagged, but nothing came of it.

"Jamie didn't realize what had happened. When the ambulance came—my mother called them after checking everything out—they found Jamie holding Willa in his arms. He was trying to stuff everything back in her head." I grimaced from the memory.

"Shut the fuck up! No way! Really?"

"Yeah." Candy shook her head. I could tell from the look in her eyes that she was recalling it, too. "Mr. Lance used to be in the National Guard. He was overseas fighting when he got called home. Ryan and Jamie stayed with Mom and me until he got home. None of them have been the same since. I kinda... I just... I felt sorry for them."

"Hell, yeah! I woulda felt like shit for them, too." Eddy ran a hand through his hair. "Fuck, man, I didn't know that shit. Sorry if I said something wrong. I—"

"It's cool, dude. Happened a long time ago." My ass was starting to hurt, so I stood up. "You still wanna hang at home?"

"Nah." Eddy scratched his chin before standing, also. "I'll come. No prob."

"I'll go, too," Candy said. "But right now, I gotta go home. Love you." She pressed her lips to mine.

"Love you, too?" I didn't mean for it to sound like a question. It just came out like that.

She giggled. "Nice to know you're not on the fence about us."

"Later, chick." Eddy bobbed and weaved like a prizefighter before playfully slugging her in the shoulder.

"Leave that shit for Tony Marchesini, Eddy." Candy rubbed her shoulder as she turned to walk away.

"Candy?" She turned when I called her name. "I do. For real. Love you, you know."

"Yeah," she said, biting her bottom lip. "I know."

"God, you guys make me sick," Eddy growled.

"Would you please," I snapped, "shut the fuck up with that shit!"

"Wow! Sorry, man. Didn't know I was bothering you." His eyes met mine, and he backed up a step. "We cool?"

"Yeah. But you need to have a little respect." It sounded far more grown up than anything else I had said in my life.

"Bye, guys." Candy waved as she walked out into the street. I followed her with my gaze, hating to see her go, but loving to watch her leave.

"Douchebag," I groaned at Eddy.

"What'd I do?"

"Just drop it." Shaking my head, I made my way up the steps to my front door. "See you tomorrow?"

"Are you mad at me, man?" Eddy sounded wounded.

"No, dude. You just... have your moments when you're an asshole. But you're my friend, so I put up with it."

"I'll try..." He stopped and scratched his head as if thinking.

"What?"

"I'll try and remember that." Eddy didn't look at me again. He just walked across the street and disappeared into his house. Maybe I had actually gotten through to him. Maybe he'd heard something like that before from some other friend in the past. Maybe, maybe, maybe.

V

When I went back inside, Jenna was picking up paper plates and red plastic party cups. She met my eyes, looked toward the kitchen and then back at me.

"You got a minute?" she asked.

"I was just about to get ready for bed, but sure." I went around the sofa and took a seat. She sat down on the coffee table across from me, letting the party favors fall to her side. One random cup landed on the floor, but she ignored it.

"How you holding up?" she asked, concern in her beautiful blue eyes.

I shrugged and rested my back against the couch. "My stitches are annoying the hell outta me. I'm getting better though. Why?"

"I was more concerned with how you're holding up against Mack Larson?" Her eyes darkened, and my blood run cold.

"What do you mean?"

"He's on you kids hard. We're supposed to call him, any of us, if we see you three around town. I mean, under no certain circumstances are we supposed to let you out of our sight."

"What are you going on about? Why would he want us watched?"

Jenna looked toward the kitchen again.

"Why are you so worried about my mother hearing you? If this is so bad, then why don't you tell someone? Mack isn't everyone's goddamn superior. If he's acting strange, then fucking report him."

"It's not that simple. Mack runs this town, Trey. I'm just worried about you kids. The last person he homed in on like this has spent the last four years upstate." She reached out and took my hands. Hers were rather cold, but I enjoyed the feel of them. I wondered what they would feel like on other parts of my body.

"What's he been saying?" I asked, trying to stay on subject.

"That you are nothing but trouble. Especially that new Treemont kid. You should've heard him when Romo attacked you. He laughed, Trey. He just laughed and said you got what you deserved." Jenna looked sad, but determined to finish her warning.

"He came to visit me in the hospital. He scared the shit out of me."

"You should be scared, Trey. He's not a good guy."

"No shit." I tried to laugh, but it just came out as nervous grumbling. "What am I supposed to do?"

"Stay far away from him. You hear me? You don't go anywhere near him. Okay?"

"We can try, but he seems to be everywhere we are."

"That's because he has everyone watching you." She shifted her weight, and the table groaned underneath her. "And I mean everyone. Not just cops, but people around town. People you don't even know."

"What about Emily Harper?" The question came out so fast I couldn't reel it back in before it escaped completely. If I wasn't careful, I would have to explain the cherry bombs.

"What about her?" Jenna seemed oblivious.

"That missing girl. Her father owns Harper's Fine Goods next to the laundromat. She's been missing for weeks."

"I don't get what she has—"

"And what are you two talking about?" Mom asked as she appeared in the doorway to the kitchen.

"Just catching up." Jenna slapped me on the knee. "Haven't seen this kid in a long time."

"I know, right?" Mom smiled. "Not since Hap's retirement party. See, that's what you get for being a stranger."

"True," Jenna said, then looked back into my eyes. "Don't worry. I'm going to be here from now on."

For the first time since the cherry bombs, I felt as though we had an adult on our side. Someone we could confide in. Still, I had to talk to Candy and Eddy before I let Jenna in on everything. God knew we needed her. I suddenly had a horrible feeling that something was about to go terribly wrong, as if my summer was going to get even worse.

Interlude 4: Innocence Lost

Among the ghosts, there are loops. They're the broken records amongst the abstract bullshit that fills my head. They aren't the dead coming back to haunt me, like Eddy. These are the memories of the lost. The ones I thought I could save, left on the wayside, forgotten. I've lost track of all of them. Some might be dead, but I'd like to think they live normal lives somewhere. All of them, save one.

There are true evils here, locked away in the safe boxes of my mind. They need to be let out, but I've misplaced the key. Where we go now, we go because I need to. There is no want involved. If I am to replace these demons with hopes of a normal future, I must delve into deeper, darker territory.

I warned you when we first started this journey that things would get nasty. Well, we've come to that juncture. You can skip this part if you like; it really doesn't matter to me at this point. Turn your head as so many others did back then. Ignore the dirty bits and move on with your life, unchanged by the course this story is about to take.

This monster we now speak of doesn't hide in the shadows or under your bed. He does not reside in any closet or attic. He lives next door. Right there, living life, being just incredibly ordinary. There is one like him in every town. He is your friend, neighbor, church member, and dinner companion. He doesn't know he is a monster. He sees nothing wrong with what he does. To him, you are the one who is different.

This is a horror show not for the faint of heart. The darkness hidden in the recesses of my mind spilled out before you. Save yourself. Because I cannot prepare you for what is to come...

Oh, Eddy, hang in there. One more mile, just one... more... mile...

Chapter Ten: Ryan and Jamie

I

July 25th, 1992

Eddy and I stood on the front lawn of the Lance's property, trying to decide why we were there. I thought we were there to visit some friends of mine I hadn't seen in a while. Eddy seemed to think it was so he could see where Willa Lance had blown off her head.

Willa Jacoby was born just nine days before my own mother. Willa was the beauty of Bay's End, a real catch to whoever made the effort. The one who finally won her was a football player named Jude Lance. There were a lot of broken hearts around town, plenty of guys thinking it should have been them. Hell, even my father dated her for a while. Why Jude had stuck was beyond anyone's guess. Yeah, he was a popular guy with a good head on his shoulders, but everyone knew he had plans of going into the Army.

The part I was never told was why Jude had finally decided on the National Guard. He was an Army man through and through, just like his dead father, who'd been killed in action during Vietnam. When the announcement was made that he was only going to be playing soldier one weekend a month and one week a year, jaws dropped all over town. Everyone just assumed he was going to be a career military man. If you asked folks back then, they might have told you Willa made him change his mind, but they would have been dead wrong.

When George Bush decided to get involved with Iraq's budding war with Kuwait in the late eighties, early nineties, the National Guard troops had been pulled in to keep the peace in less hostile areas of Saudi Arabia. Corporal Jude Lance had been one of those.

Bay's End sent him off with a gala that took up all of Rifle Park. They even lit the bonfire early that year. Like Hap Carringer's retirement party, drunk adults and meandering kids were everywhere. It was, for all intents and purposes, a fun time.

The twins, Ryan and Jamie, hated to see their father go. He was sent off with slobbery kisses and vice-like hugs. He promised them when he came back that everything would be all right again. They would go to Disney World down in Florida. It would be more fun than they'd ever had.

None of that ever happened. Jude was brought home to bury his wife just eighteen months later.

"Was it like half her head, or like, you know, the entire top of her head?" Eddy asked.

"Dude!"

"What?" Eddy shrugged. "It's a simple question."

"You're sick." I shoved him away from me.

"Whatever." Eddy straightened his shirt where I'd messed it up and began walking for the porch. I followed.

We stood in front of the door, waiting for each other to knock, before I finally sighed and rapped my knuckles on the screen. Waiting was not a strong point for either of us, and we constantly changed positions, putting our hands in our jeans pockets, then removing them a second later. We weren't nervous so much as just fidgety.

Ryan opened the door what seemed like an hour later. He was bare-chested, and his belt hung open in front of his crotch. "What's up?" He wiped something from his mouth.

"Wanna hang out?" Eddy asked, giving Ryan the bucks.

"I can't go anywhere. Dad's asleep. But you guys can come in if you want." Ryan stepped to the side, and we walked into the foyer.

The hall was set up like a showcase. Jude Lance held an affinity for die-cast replicas of old cars and service vehicles. Three rows of display cases stood along the walls of the short hallway. Old Hudson police cruisers from the forties, Number 11 fire engines constructed to the tiniest detail, an old Packard Ambulance that looked more like a classic milk truck than something EMTs would drive. He also had a '67 Corvette with D-cup wheel wells, an old Ford F-150 with wood panels, a Woody with a miniature surf board on the roof, and a solid gold casting of a '20s hearse.

"That shit is rad, man," Eddy exclaimed. "Your old man make this shit?"

"Most of it. He used to, anyway. Now he just polishes and tends to what he has. He focuses on... other things now." Ryan looked at the cars distantly, as if they were fading images on a big screen at the old Paramount Theater.

"Well, they're fucking cool," Eddy assured him.

"Come on." Ryan waved us out of the hallway and into the living area.

We heard Mr. Lance snoring before we actually saw him. He lay on the couch in the front room, naked aside from a pair of boxers, the head of his penis lolling from the opening. I diverted my eyes quickly. It wasn't something I wanted to see. Ryan, noticing why I was looking away, placed a throw pillow over his father's crotch and hid the limp thing from view.

On the television screen, a blond woman was on her hands and knees, her ass glowing red from too many slaps, while a buff guy in a mailman's uniform rammed her from behind. Though he was fully clothed, his engorged member protruded from his open fly to delve into the woman's glistening slit. In, out. In, out.

"What the hell?" Eddy smiled wider than I'd ever seen. He put his palms on the back of the sofa and leaned forward over Mr. Lance's sleeping form. Eddy slid his glasses up his nose to get a better view of the TV. "And I thought my old man was fucking cool. Jesus, man!"

"Holy shit," I stammered. I'd never seen a real life porno. Sure, I'd caught the late-night stroke flicks on Skinemax, but they didn't show half that much. "Your dad just leaves this shit playing?"

"No big deal." Ryan raised his shoulders and let them fall as though watching porn was just an everyday occurrence. "He gets his rocks off and falls to sleep. Least he leaves us alone when he's watching it."

The statement hung on the air, neither Eddy or I noticing what had been said. We didn't see the meaning there. We were two preteen boys watching a major fuck-fest unfold before our eyes. Ryan could have told us the Russians were on his front porch, that World War Three had started, and we would have just continued watching that blonde getting hammered.

"Hey." Ryan scared both of us out of our adolescent trance with his sudden outburst. "You guys want to play hide and go seek?"

"Huh?" Eddy asked, still glued to the porn.

"Sure, I guess." I looked away from the television for the first time since laying eyes on it. I could feel my dick straining against my zipper, but figured if I ignored it and got my mind on something else, the hard-on would eventually go away. "Where?"

"In the house. Around the backyard. All over, really."

"Huh?" Eddy grumbled again, not really paying attention.

"Sounds good." I elbowed Eddy.

He turned to look at me. "What? Shit, man, can't you see—"

"We're gonna play hide and go seek, asshole. You're playing." It was a statement, not a question.

"Oh, yeah, sure thing." Eddy's eyes reverted back to the screen, and he licked his lips.

The mailman's money-shot arced across the blonde's back and crack. Eddy finally turned away from the television. "Remind me to ask your old man to borrow that flick. I give it three big thumbs up." Eddy raised his thumbs, jutting his crotch out for us to see the bulge there.

"You're fucking sick." I shook my head, laughing.

"I'm just a man, man!" Eddy rotated his hand, turning his thumbs-up into an upright middle finger. That obscene gesture was becoming a term of endearment. "So, where're we playing?"

"We'll start in the backyard," Ryan said, looking happy. I could only imagine he didn't get much fun, being stuck in the house all the time. "Jamie's out there playing in the dirt, but he might want to play."

"It's going to be easy finding him," Eddy said. I jabbed him in the ribs with my elbow. "What?"

"Be nice, asshole. Jesus, you kill me with that shit," I said.

"You'd be surprised, Eddy," Ryan said. "My brother is pretty good at hide-and-go-seek."

"We'll see. I hold the crown, or so I've been told." Eddy hitched a thumb at Mr. Lance on the couch. "We gonna disturb sleeping ugly over here?"

"Not likely," Ryan said. "He sleeps pretty good after... ya know."

"Yeah." Eddy nudged me, winking. "We know."

But, truth was, we didn't know.

II

We found Jamie out back covered in dirt and grass. His over-large head held a mischievous grin that stretched from ear to ear. The gap in his front teeth showed a thick tongue trying to poke through. An excavated patch of green lay atop his head, and clods of dirt dripped like fat rain drops.

"Trey-day!" he roared in that wet way of his, drool and spittle flying. His heavy legs pushed him up off the ground and carried him over to me. A clump of damp earth, like a drying mud-pie, lay in his left hand. He offered it to me, and I declined, respectfully.

"Wanna play hide and seek, Jay?" Ryan asked. Though they were twins, they couldn't have been more different in appearance. Other than the fact that Jamie had Down's Syndrome and all the characteristics that came with the affliction, he was a good half a foot taller than his "older" brother. Ryan had brown hair, Jamie blond. Jamie's thick upper body made Ryan look bird-chested in comparison. Not to mention, Jamie's far superior hygiene. Ryan, you would have thought, would be the cleaner of the two, but that was far from the case. Though Jamie was the one covered in dirt from a day of playing, Ryan smelled as if he hadn't showered in weeks. A mixed odor of urine and sweat came off him in waves. So much so, I was almost unable to stand within five feet of him.

Jamie bounced up and down, clapping his hands happily as he belted, "Hide un peek! Hide un peek!"

Eddy laughed. "It's hide and seek."

"He can't say it right. Don't try," I said.

"Dotta get a churt on, Ry," Jamie said as he tweaked his brother's nipple.

Ryan didn't seem to mind. Eddy and I shared a look, but then, we both shrugged.

"Right," Ryan said. "Be right back!"

"You donna see my bubberflies today, Trey-day?" Jamie asked.

"After the game, okay?"

"Yeppers." Jamie spit when he pronounced the Ps, but I had already shielded my face, just in case. The saliva ran down the back of my hand in rivulets. "I dotta find more, Trey-day. Dey's all dead now." He cast his face to the ground. "Dotta do somethin' to keep dem live and swell."

"Alive and well," Eddy said, shaking his head.

"Give him a break, asshole," I hissed at Eddy.

"Sorry, man, I can't help it."

"Back!" Ryan called as he stormed from the back door. "Like it?" He wore a black T-shirt with frayed ends where the sleeves had been cut off. On the front, reminding me of the shirts Eddy wore, were big yellow letters that read, "Ladies Man!" He spun around and showed us the back: "A Skirt Will Get You Everywhere!"

I didn't quite understand the shirt, but I ignored it. I half-expected Eddy to say he liked it, but he only shook his head with a confused look on his face. He glanced at me, and I shrugged.

"You dies ready?" Jamie asked, looking as though he might burst. Spontaneous combustion seemed perfectly plausible with the way he was bounding around. His face was red from his efforts. "I really dood at dis dame, dies."

"I remember," I told him.

"Who's going first?" Ryan asked.

"Tag!" Eddy slapped me on the shoulder. "You're it, fucker!"

All three of them took off running, Jamie slower than the other two, lurching forward in that bow-legged gait of his, wailing and screaming gleefully the entire way.

"Tount, Trey-day!" Jamie yelled. "Tount to twenty!"

"Close your eyes, shithead!" Eddy hollered as he ran around the side of the house. "Shut 'em!"

I turned around and placed my forearm over my eyes. Slowly, I began to count, one... two... three... all the way up to twenty. I heard Jamie's muffled laughter fade as the screen door on the back of the house slammed shut. Footfalls could be located off to my left, but they soon stopped around the side of the house. I was sure that was where Eddy was, as he had been headed in that direction before I closed my peepers. I had no clue where Ryan had gone, though.

As I hit twenty, I spun around, yelling, "Come out, come out, wherever you are!" and was welcomed by an empty backyard.

I slunk off to the right. As I came around the side of the house, I noticed two blue trash bins and a large heating and cooling unit. The scene wasn't all that different from where I'd been attacked by Romo and I felt my heart beat a little faster as memories flooded.

I steeled myself and opened the first trashcan. Empty. So was the other one. I sighed. That was where I would have hidden.

Sneaking around the side of the AC unit, I peeked over the edge, but found no one there. Eddy might have run around the front of the house, but there was nowhere to hide up there. Yet, nothing would have stopped him from going through the front door and hiding somewhere in the house.

I crept around to the front yard and scanned the area. Mr. Lance's blue minivan sat in the driveway. I circled it just to make sure no one was hiding there, and finished off my search by looking under it, too.

The only place left was inside the house.

Walking lightly across the front porch, I pulled open the screen door and found the front door slightly ajar. I laid my palm against it, and it opened quietly enough. I couldn't remember whether or not Ryan had closed it after us—what with the porno show going on—so I didn't focus on that too long.

Scanning the living room, I found no one, aside from Mr. Lance still snoring on the sofa. A new scene was being played out on the TV. A young black girl was on her knees in front of a man with a massive erect penis. The term "mushroom lollipop" popped into my head, and I smiled. I'd have to remember that one for another day.

I left the front room and made my way through the door of the kitchen. The area was way too quiet. I normally used my hearing to place ragged breathing and catch the slightest of movements, but I couldn't hear anything as I made my way through the dining area. I checked the pantry and found hundreds of cans and boxed dinners. There was absolutely no room for anyone to be hiding there. I closed the door and went to the fridge. I opened the heavy door of the Frigidaire—leftovers in Tupperware, egg cartons, and a half-gallon of milk. I checked the cupboards under the sink, under the tablecloth that hung to the floor—noting that as a possible hiding place for myself when it came to be my turn—and crazily, even the freezer unit on the far wall.

Eddy scared the shit out of me when I opened the lid of the deep freeze and found him shivering inside.

"Damn it," he grumbled.

I slapped him across the arm. "You're it, fucker! Olly olly oxen free!" I called, not even thinking I might wake up Mr. Lance.

"Shit," Ryan moaned as he came out of the bathroom, shaking his head. "That was way too quick."

"S-s-sorry." Eddy shivered as he pulled himself out of the freezer unit. "I couldn't f-f-f-find anywhere else to huh-hide." He wrapped his arms around himself and rubbed his biceps. "Th-that was a st-st-stupid idea."

I laughed. "Yeah, it was."

"Fuh-fuck you, m-m-m-man," he stammered.

"Dat was fad," Jamie said as he stumbled out of the hallway. I couldn't tell where he had been hiding. Probably one of the bedrooms, but I didn't know for sure.

"Ready for round two?" Ryan asked.

"I guess so," Eddy huffed. "Damn, that was cold."

"It's a fucking freezer, dude," I said.

"No shit? Really? Thank you, Captain Oblivious."

"It's Captain Obvious, stupid," I corrected him.

Eddy flipped me off. "How about Captain Fuck-off?"

"Whatever." I put an arm around him and pretended to brush something off his shoulder. "It's your turn."

"Yeah, yeah. I'm going." Eddy pulled away from me.

"Out back with you." I kicked him in the ass as he walked away. "I promise I won't hide in the freezer."

"Me, neither," Ryan called after him.

"Me, deeder!" Jamie spit.

III

We scurried like cockroaches after the lights had been turned on. Ryan made for his own bedroom, Jamie went for the front yard, and I bolted for Mr. Lance's room. I slid onto my stomach and low-crawled under his four-post bed.

Even though the house was cool, sweat instantly broke out across my forehead. I was breathing harder than I wanted to and trying to hold it so as to stay quiet, but that only made it worse. I drew the back of my hand across my brow, and it came back soaked.

I heard the back screen door squeak open, and my breath caught in my throat. I tried to remain still, quiet, but my lungs were starting to burn. Exhaling sharply, then hissing loudly as I drew in fresh air, I tried to calm myself.

Eddy's heavy footsteps gave away his location in the hallway. He certainly wasn't taking the stealthy route. Because of my ragged breathing, I was certain he would find me at any moment. I sounded like a fuming bull to my own ears.

Eddy stalked through the door of Mr. Lance's bedroom. His brown Nikes slid across the carpet in my field of vision. *Why'd he have to come in here first?* my brain yelled. I watched as he moved over to the closet and opened it. An avalanche of dirty, musty-smelling laundry flooded out around his feet. He cussed loudly and bent to push everything back in. A stray sock smelling of expired corn chips landed near my head. I curled my nose away from the funk, but the odor made its way into my mouth and to the back of my throat. I couldn't take it anymore and let out my pent-up breath.

Luckily, at the same time, Eddy cursed, so he didn't hear me sucking wind. I took three more shallow breaths before holding it again. The foul taste rolling over my tongue was gag-inducing, but I was able to hold back.

Eddy snatched up the horrible smelling sock without looking under the bed and tossed it back on top of the pile of laundry. After kicking the closet door closed, he left the room as loudly as he'd entered. With the filthy sock gone, I was finally able to breathe fresh air. Even though the odor lingered, wonderful oxygen filled my body, and my upset stomach subsided. I didn't think I would have lasted much longer. Thank God for Eddy's impatience.

I spotted the corner of a Polaroid peeking out of a tear in the bottom of the box spring. The telltale white border gave it away. Finding it rather strange that a picture would have been stuck in the bottom of a mattress, I plucked it from its confines with my thumb and forefinger. Studying the odd photo, it took me a minute to realize what the image was.

Jamie stood in his room—I could tell from the poster of Howard the Duck over his right shoulder—completely naked. He was smiling his goofy smile at the camera. The tiny head of his limp penis stuck out from the grasp of his fist. His other hand was behind him as if he were about to take a bow.

243

My stomach turned, and my mind reeled. I couldn't think of one possible explanation for that picture. Why would someone take a nude photo of a mentally challenged child? Why would someone possibly need something like that? Questions spun in my gray matter, but there was not a single answer anywhere in there.

I decided it would be best if I just put the picture back where I'd found it, but then, I heard a *Thud!* from across the hall.

"Fucking faggot!" Eddy's voice was muffled, but I understood every word. "Nasty fucker!"

Thud! I realized I was hearing someone being slammed against a wall.

Thud!

"Jesus," I mumbled as I pulled myself out from under the bed. Eddy was screaming, enraged. I'd never heard him like that. I pushed myself up once I was clear from under the bed and took off for where the sounds were coming from.

Almost passing Ryan's room, I slid to a halt out in the hall when I heard Ryan scream, "Get your hands off me!"

I burst into Ryan's room and stopped. Shock and fright stole away all semblance of reality.

Ryan was cowering in the corner of his closet, his pants and briefs around his ankles. His hands were drawn up to his chin as if in a defensive pose. Just outside the closet door, Eddy stood with his arms at his sides. At the end of each arm was a balled-up fist. His cheeks were bright red, and he was shaking like a leaf. The front of his shirt rose and fell quickly as he took shallow breaths.

"Help, Trey. He's crazy," Ryan whined, tears on his cheeks.

"This fucking queer asked me to suck his dick," Eddy growled.

"What?" I asked.

"I did not!" Ryan said. "I didn't. I swear!"

Eddy turned and met my eyes with his crazed vision. "I came in here and checked the closet, and this ass monkey—"

"He's lying!"

"—had his pants round his ankles with his cock in his hand—"

"I didn't!"

"—asking me if I wanted to put my mouth on him!" Eddy finished with a roar. He took a step forward and raised a fist.

"Eddy!" I grabbed his shoulder.

"What the fuck, man?" Eddy whipped around, but he lowered his fist. I was actually surprised he didn't swing at me. "I don't do that gay shit, Trey!"

"Just leave him alone," I said. "He's about to wet himself, he's so scared. Look at him."

"I don't gotta look at him, Trey. Trust me. I saw enough of him."

"What's going on in here?" Mr. Lance said, showing himself in the doorway of Ryan's room.

"Oddy oddy oxfree!" Jamie bellowed as he bounced up behind his father, grinning and drooling.

"Nothing. But your boy's a little cock polisher." Eddy puffed out his chest as if to prove he was all man. He just looked silly, though.

"Aw, Ryan." Mr. Lance dropped his head. "What did I say about playing without me?"

Both Eddy and I looked at Mr. Lance in about the exact same way. Confusion mixed with a bit of 'what-the-fuck-did-you-just-say?'.

"Come on, boys." Mr. Lance smiled. "Who doesn't like a little fun?"

"Fucking great." Eddy sighed, lowering his head.

"Let's have a few drinks. You boys drink, don't you? Even if you don't—"

"Move it, fucker," Eddy hissed as he shoved Mr. Lance hard in the gut and out of the doorway. Mr. Lance fell into the wall of the hallway and groaned. I quickly followed Eddy as he headed toward the front door.

"Guess drinks are out of the question, then." Mr. Lance chuckled behind us. "This stays between us, boys!" he called as we ran out of the front door.

IV

My father looked at us strangely when we came busting into the living room. I snatched the cordless off its base as I walked toward the kitchen. I dialed 911 and screwed the handset to my ear. As I listened to the ringing on the other end, I felt something running down my right leg. Pulling up my pants leg with my free hand, I saw blood seeping from my bandage down into my shoe. I made a mental note to take care of that after I took care of Mr. Lance.

"Bay's End Emergency Services, how can I direct your call?" Jenna sounded bored. Well, I was about to change that.

"Jenna, it's Trey Franklin," I yelled into the phone. "I need a cop, like quick."

"What's going on, Trey?" my father asked as he came into the kitchen. "You're bleeding." He pointed at my leg.

I nodded at him, but spoke into the phone. "We got a problem at the Lance's house down the street."

"Trey, are you all right?" Jenna asked.

"Yeah, I'm fine, but his boys aren't." I stopped to catch my breath. "He's been fooling with them, Jenna. Taking naked pictures and... doing things."

"What's going on, Eddy?" my dad asked.

"Just listen," Eddy told him, pointing at me.

"What? Mr. Lance is?" Jenna sounded confused.

"Yes!" I huffed. "I found this picture of Jamie butt-naked under Jude Lance's bed, and Eddy almost got raped by Ryan."

"Wait," Eddy said, looking at my dad who was now wide-eyed, looking at him. "That's not entirely true."

"Mr. Lance?" Jenna asked.

"For Christ's sake, Jenna, fucking yes!" I looked at my dad, but he didn't even seem to notice the language.

"All right, Trey, sorry, I just don't—"

"Just get someone over there. I'll fill them in when they get here. Promise," I begged.

"Did he... touch you?" she asked.

"No!" I said, exasperated. "Just get a car out here, okay?"

"On their way."

"Good."

"And Trey?"

"Yeah?"

"Be careful."

"Why?"

"It's gonna be Mack responding."

I almost dropped the phone. "Great," I moaned.

"Just be on point, Trey."

"Gotcha." I hung up the phone.

"One of you mind telling me what the hell is going on?" Dad asked as he sat down next to me at the table.

"Eddy," I said, meeting his eyes.

"Yeah?"

"Will you get my bandages and stuff from my room while I fill Dad in?"

Eddy nodded and ran down the hall.

"Did he touch you?" Dad asked, looking as if he might cry.

"Nah. It didn't get that far. We were playing hide and seek, and…" I filled Dad in, relating everything I could remember. He sat there, his jaw slack as he listened. Dad never interrupted. Not once did he question a thing I was telling him. I should have thanked him for that.

V

I would absolutely love to tell you Officer Mack showed up and did his duty, that he led Jude Lance away in handcuffs and everything was all hunky-dory. But, nothing was ever that simple when Mack Larson was involved.

I watched him park his cruiser out front. He strode up our walk, taking off his hat and stuffing it under his arm, his scar catching the dying light of the day, his cheek working with what I could only assume was another cough drop, cherry-flavored, of course. The knocking came loud and thunderous, as if *we* were the criminals.

Eddy had just finished downing a can of Coke from the fridge. His face flushed red as he started coughing.

Dad yelled, "Hang on!" as he finished my bandage and tossed the bloody one in the wastebasket. He went to the door.

"What seems to be the problem?" Mack shined that smile of his. Dad would assume it was just a symbol of courtesy, but Eddy and I knew better.

"Ask the boys. They're the ones with all the answers," Dad said, hitching his chin in my direction. Eddy's coughing fit subsided, and he joined me on the couch. He looked so pale, he might as well of seen a ghost. That was one of the few times I ever saw fear in his eyes.

Mack stood even after Dad offered him a place to sit in his recliner. I could tell he liked the position of power that came with looking down on us.

"Problems?" Officer Mack asked, taking a tablet out of his breast pocket. The pad of paper was tiny in his bear paw, but in mine, it would have taken up the entire length of my hand.

"It's Mr. Lance, sir." The *sir* came out low, as if it were a naughty word. A vision of a burnt husk of a cherry bomb flitted into my vision, and I swallowed hard. I looked over at Eddy. His hands were shaking in his lap. "We found some stuff."

"Yep." Mack nodded. "What kinda stuff, Trey?" Not Franklin, not son, but *Trey*. He was acting strangely, and in the back of my mind, I knew it was because my father was there. Mack was wearing his mask. I'd seen it before, but never up close. If I hadn't known better, I'd have thought he really wanted to help us.

"Naked pictures of Jamie... holding himself." I shivered, remembering the nasty photo.

"Really?" Was that shock playing across his face? It looked real enough.

I nodded.

Eddy jumped in. "We were playing hide and go seek, you know, just chillin' and stuff, when I found Ryan in the closet with his pants down. He wanted me to... put my mouth on him. At least, that's what he said." Eddy swallowed hard, and I saw his tiny Adam's apple fight to bob back to the surface.

"Hm," Mack grumbled as he jotted something in his notebook. "Ryan Lance said this?"

"Yes, sir." Eddy mirrored my earlier manners. In no other light would we ever have called that man "sir," but if Mack wanted to play goody-two-shoes, we would play along.

"Then Mr. Lance came in and said something about playing with us. He offered us drinks, too." My words came out fast, jumbled, and for a moment, I thought he hadn't heard me.

"That's some serious accusin' you two got goin' on." Mack eyed us, the eye above the scar squinting a little more than the other. "You could ruin a man with accusin' like this. You boys know that, right?"

"Yes, sir," we said in unison.

"Since we can't prove these things were said—your words 'gainst his, you understand—we'll focus on the photograph. Where was this picture?"

"Under his bed. I hid there while Eddy was searching for us. I found it sticking out from the box springs. It was just... there." That last part came out of my mouth sounding way too silly for my liking.

"You gonna look into this tonight?" Dad asked. He was still standing by the front door, leaning on the wall of the foyer. "If what the boys are saying is true, those boys of Jude's are in some trouble."

Mack nodded. "I'll look into it. I don't think it will be tonight, you understand."

"What?" Eddy and I both burst off the couch.

"Calm down," Mack started.

"I don't see any reason to wait," Dad said. He didn't look a bit happy, but he was nowhere as upset as Eddy and I were.

"This is fucking stupid!" Eddy blurted.

"Watch the language, son." That was the Mack we knew, if only in a flash, but he was there nonetheless, just waiting. His face changed to one of patience, the true Mack once more hidden behind the mask. "These things take time. I need to be able to talk to the Lance boys when their father isn't around. I have to get social services involved—"

"Fuck that, you procrastinating shit! Do something!" Eddy roared, balling his fists at his sides.

"Eddy," Dad warned.

Mack was loving every minute of Eddy's outburst. That smile crept over his face; his scar lifted and his eyes gleamed. I suddenly had a horrible feeling Mack was baiting Eddy. He wanted him to react that way.

"Eddy." I put a hand on his shoulder. "Calm down."

Eddy ripped away from me. "If you don't do something, well, I guess I'll have to have my father handle him. Dad don't like people who fuck with little kids."

"Oh, now you wouldn't want to do that, Ed," Mack said, shaking his head. "Your father could go to jail. I'd hate to drag him downtown for an assault charge."

"I bet you *would* fucking hate it," Eddy hissed. "You'd love every damn minute of it."

"Curb the language, son, or I'll have to—"

"Sorry." Eddy put his hands up in front of him, feigning fright. "Pardon my French, right? I say that bit, and it's all better, right? Just like Officer Mack. Be a good little boy, and all is forgiven. Or what? I get bent over your hood again?"

"Shut your friend up, Franklin," Mack said. His breathing was growing ragged, and the smell of cherries and menthol covered my face. There was a moment when the hatred in Mack's eyes overplayed the need for the mask, and I was sure he would crack. That scar would peel open, the real man would finally show himself, and my father would behold Mack Larson in all his terrible ferocity.

"What's he talking about?" Dad asked, looking confused.

My father's words seemed to reel Mack back in from the edge. The officer sighed, probably realizing how close he'd come to giving himself away.

"Oh, nothing." Mack shot my father that smile. "Eddy and I had a little disagreement about playing out at the Westerns. I thought I would take him in for trespassing, but decided home would be better. Haven't been out there since, have you, Eddy?"

"Fuck this." Eddy threw up his hands and pushed past me, heading for the door. "I'll catch you tomorrow, Trey."

"I got his statement. Let him go," Mack said when he saw me about to move for Eddy. "You can fill in the blanks."

"What blanks?" I asked. My hands were shaking, and I jumped when Eddy slammed the door behind him.

"Did he… touch *you*?" Mack asked without looking at me. He stared down at his notebook, clicking the end of his pen in and out.

I shook my head. "No, he didn't have a chance."

"Do you still have that picture?"

I fought to remember what the hell I had done with it. Eddy's throwing Ryan around had caught me in the moment. I remembered that I was about to put it back, but… "No. I don't remember what happened to it."

Mack smiled, "Well, if you remember, you call me." He handed me a card with his contact info on it. "You call me... personally. Ya hear?"

"Yeah, sure." I stuffed the card in my back pocket and looked at my dad. He looked none too happy.

"You're sure you can't go at least talk to him tonight?" Dad asked Mack, his arms across his chest.

"These things are delicate, Mr. Franklin."

"Please. Call me Danny."

"Okay, then. These cases are really fragile, Danny. One wrong move, one small piece of bad info—not that the boys are lying, you see—and the entire case goes down the tubes. Wouldn't want it to go bad and him walk. If he is guilty, ya know."

"I kinda see where that could hurt everything in the end." Dad didn't sound convinced, and I was happy to see the doubt in his eyes.

"I guess that's everything, then." Mack flipped his patrolman's cap back onto his head. "You gentlemen have a good night. Oh, and Trey?"

"Yeah." I looked up to meet those deep brown eyes.

"Best if you steer clear of over there, ya hear?" He tipped his hat at me as he left. It was a sight I would never erase from my memory. He was warning me, but not about Mr. Lance. It was an all-encompassing warning. *Stay out of trouble, you little shit. Pardon my French, o' course.*

Dad sighed as he closed the door behind Mack. "I don't believe this."

"He's not going to do anything, Dad. I promise you, he's not."

"I know, Trey," Dad said, and I could see the sadness in his eyes. "I don't know what it is about that guy, but he thoroughly gives me the fucking creeps."

"Ditto," I breathed as I looked through the window and watched Mack drive away.

"You just stay clear of everything, Trey, the Lances, Mack, all of them. If we don't hear something back from Mack in the next few days, we'll call Jenna and go higher up than Mack Larson. Deal?" Dad looked very no-nonsense, and I liked seeing that on him. He looked strong, powerful. It was comforting.

"Deal."

VI

With the day behind me, I was finally able to settle down for a minute. Mom got home from her evening shopping—she'd been at Peaton's Grocery the entire time Eddy and I were discovering the truth behind Ryan, Jamie, and Mr. Lance—and I filled her in as I helped her unload the groceries.

Her face kept changing from fear to shock to worry, but the end result was anger. "That man... something needs to be done about that man," Mom told Dad as I loaded the fridge with fresh eggs and cauliflower.

"Mack said he'd look into it." Dad shook his head.

"Why isn't he doing something now?" Mom grabbed a jar of peanut butter and slung it into the cabinet above the stove.

"He said it was a 'delicate' situation," Dad said.

"He must not have believed you, Trey. This really did happen, right?"

"I swear on everything, Mom." I performed the Boy Scout salute, even though I had never even set foot in a troop. "He even offered us drinks."

"Just sick," Mom huffed, laying a hand over her heart. "I'm talking to Jenna tomorrow and see if there is anything she can suggest."

"Sounds good," Dad agreed.

"Really?" I asked. "You'll do that?"

"I don't see any other choice in the matter." Mom's was the final word on the subject.

Dad and I both nodded. I was beginning to see more and more similarities between the two of us. It wasn't all that bad, either.

"And you have no idea where you left that picture of Jamie?" Mom asked, checking my eyes for the truth.

"Honest." I crossed my heart. "I'm sorry. I was just kinda... you know..."

"It's not your fault, Trey," Dad said. The corner of his mouth lifted in a sad smile. "There's nothing you could have done different. It's time for the adults to handle things now."

"I know." I sighed. "It's just, you know, kinda fuh-uh, screwed up." I'd been hanging around Eddy too much, and his mouth was going to me in trouble if I wasn't careful. I chose my next words very carefully. "What makes a man want to... you know... mess with kids?"

Mom and Dad looked at each other, my question weighing heavy on the air. Mom nodded at Dad, and he turned back to look at me.

"Some people, Trey, are just broken."

And that was it. It was the best response, really. It would take me years to understand my father's words, but that didn't change the fact that he was as right then as he would have been now. Some people didn't have that switch, that wall, that whatever the hell you wanted to call it. Some people were just bad for no reason. There was nothing you could do about it.

That night, I dreamt of being chased again. But there was more than just Romo on my heels.

The hallway was familiar. It was the short hall in the foyer of Mr. Lance's house. The car replicas sat lonely on forgotten shelves. Hundreds of spiders had made their homes under each one. Webs dangling like discarded silk doilies. Footsteps thundered behind me. The sounds of wet snarls were followed by a voice, hissing and sinister.

"What did I say about playing without me?"

My screams echoed off the walls. My chest burned with lack of oxygen and thudded with my drumming heart. I could feel the spittle on the back of my neck from Romo's barks and growls. Reaching back, my hand came away wet.

"This stays between us, boys!"

They caught me.

I woke up covered in sweat and blood. Grasped in my hand like a rag doll was a soiled bandage. I reached for the back of my neck and felt my sticky stitches. My hand came away red.

Mom found me washing my hands in the bathroom. She checked out the back of my neck and said I hadn't torn anything loose. As she bandaged me back up, her eyes looked distant in the bathroom mirror.

"I'm sorry all this happened to you today," she whispered.

"Not your fault." I grimaced as the bandage caught one of my stitches and pulled.

"I know. But you've been through so much lately. First that damn dog, now this." She started to cry. "I just wish I could've been there for you. But this damn job and—"

"Mom... it's okay."

She swallowed me in her arms. We cried. I was sure she needed it more than I did.

Chapter Eleven: Revelations

I

July 26th, 1992

Eddy showed up at my front door just before eleven o'clock the next morning. He looked like shit. Granted, he had a reason, but he also had something that would take both of our minds off stuff for a while.

"*Wayne's World* is playing down at the Paramount. Fifty-cent showing any time before five," he said as he showed me a handful of quarters.

"Really?" I smiled. "That thing came out like back in March."

"February, actually. That's why it's showing for a half dollar." He jingled the change in his hand and flashed his bucks. "Got enough for Sanders and Candice if you want to ask them."

"Sure thing," I told him as I went to the phone.

I dialed Sanders number, but all I got was a busy signal. Candy's phone was no different. I looked at Eddy and shrugged as I put the cordless back on the base.

"Their lines are busy," I said.

"We can always stop by their houses on the way."

"True."

"You ready?"

"Lemme go tell Mom and Dad where we're going."

"Okay," Eddy said, crashing down on the couch. "You got the right stuff... baby," he sang as I went to find my parents.

Mom was in her room, gathering clothes for laundry. I asked her if I could go, and she reminded me to be home by dark, then as an afterthought, told me to tell my father where I was going, too. I didn't bother telling her I'd planned on doing that anyway.

Dad was trimming the branches off the oak in the middle of our backyard. He looked hot and sweaty, even though the day was rather cool for mid-summer.

"Mind if I go to see *Wayne's World* at the Paramount?" I called out the back door.

"Sure," Dad said, wiping his glistening brow on his bare forearm.

"Sure... you mind?"

"Nah, sorry," he huffed. "Just be home by dark."

I laughed. "Yeah. Mom told me."

"Then, why are you bothering me?" He grinned. "Go on. Just stay away from you-know-who."

"No doubt. Bye!"

"Later," he called as I made my way back through the house.

"All's fine?" Eddy asked as I took off for the door.

"Last one there," I challenged.

"Shithead," Eddy growled and pushed himself off the couch.

We ran outside headed toward Candy's house. The sun was just peeking over the trees in the distance, taking its sweet time getting the day started. Ignoring the pull of the stitches in my right leg, hoping they wouldn't bust on me, I bounded up the steps of Candy's house.

Huffing and puffing, I laid fist to door and waited as Eddy popped up beside me.

"You're gonna rip that leg of yours open," he said, not even out of breath.

"I'll deal." I knocked again.

"Candice!" Eddy called. I moved away from him. He'd yelled right in my ear.

The door opened, and I immediately knew something was wrong. Candy's eyes were downcast, looking at my Nikes, and she wore nothing but an extra-large pink shirt with a brown stain between her breasts. Her pale legs stuck out of the makeshift nightgown, and I could see she'd cut herself shaving. Two red pieces of toilet paper stuck to her inner thigh and mid-calf.

"You okay?" I asked.

"Yeah, sure," she lied.

"What's wrong?" Eddy asked, wiping sweat off his neck.

"Just been busy."

"In your PJs?" Eddy laughed.

She raised her head and snapped, "No!"

"Calm down, chick, sheesh. What's your deal?"

"Eddy, shut up." I asked Candy, "You feel like hanging out?"

"Nah." She started playing with her hands, scrubbing them together as if they were dirty or something. "I got some... things to do. Maybe tomorrow?"

"It's *Wayne's World*," Eddy whined. "It's on at the cheap seats. Come on."

"I just can't. Bye, guys." She shut the door in our faces.

"Well, that was awkward. What'd you do to her?" Eddy asked as we left the porch.

"I didn't do anything to her. She's just acting weird."

"You're telling me." He laughed. "I guess Sanders is next."

"What time does the movie start?" I stepped out into the street and headed for Lime.

"Just after noon. We got plenty of time." Eddy sneezed and wiped it on his jeans.

"Getting sick?"

"Allergies or some shit. I hope Sanders ain't fucking busy. Seeing this thing with you as my date ain't my idea of fun," Eddy said as we turned onto Fir.

"You know what?"
"What?"
"Fuck you."
"Yo momma."

II

Eddy and I thundered up the front porch of Sanders's house, stomping loudly to announce our arrival. Sulan's BMW wasn't in the driveway, but I was sure someone was home. His phone had been busy.

"Sanders!" Eddy screamed, his voice cracking from the strain. I hadn't even had the chance to knock yet.

"Would you please quit with that shit. Have you ever heard of just waiting for someone to answer a door?" I growled, covering my ears.

"Sorry, sheesh." Eddy dropped his head and kicked his foot at nothing in particular. I gave the dude a lot of shit, but he normally gave it right back.

We heard Sanders's heavy footfalls as he made his way through the house. He was talking in whatever language his father spoke, and Eddy and I found that fact funny for some reason. I thought he sounded like one of those old kung fu movies that came on Sunday mornings.

When Sanders finally opened the door, he had a handset pressed to the side of his head. He held it there with his shoulder while he opened the door wide enough for both of us to enter. We followed his gaze to the living room and took a seat in front of his over-large projection television set.

The walls were covered with 3D oriental artwork. One painting in particular looked as though it had moving parts. Water cascaded over a waterfall while a small village lay at the precipice of a cliff side. Upon further inspection, I found that it was actually just a play of lighting behind the canvas that gave off the effect. It was kind of cool to watch. Hypnotizing, even.

The fireplace mantle was covered in jade figures of elephants and an eight-armed goddess. There were family pictures of time spent in Sulan's native country, a trip to Knott's Berry

Farm out in California, and an awards gala that I had actually attended with Sanders. The ceremony was for a writing contest in which Sanders had won first place and I'd received an honorable mention. Rather strangely, I ended up being the writer.

Sanders hollered something in that foreign tongue, and I jumped.

"And a Hong Kong fooey to you tooey," Eddy whispered, snickering.

"Hush, dude." But I couldn't help but laugh, too.

I heard the beep of his cordless as the call was ended, and Sanders flopped down on the love seat next to the couch where Eddy and I sat. "Hey-Zues, my father is a pain."

"You got a really nice place, man." Eddy surveyed the room as he spoke. "Really Japped out, but really nice."

"Japped out?" Sanders looked at me for help with the term.

"He's just an idiot. Forget him." I elbowed Eddy in the ribs, but it didn't seem to faze him. "So, you wanna go see *Wayne's World* at the Mount?"

"Can't."

"Dammit. Why not?" Eddy grumbled.

"'Cause of this bullcrud." Sanders reached into his front pocket. He slid down the cushion a bit to do so, but after a little struggle, he straightened with his fist clenched. "Wanna tell me why this was on my porch this morning?" Sanders chucked the object in his hand at Eddy.

Both Eddy and I stopped breathing for a moment. The air was heavy with tension. The thing in Eddy's lap had a gravity all its own as it pulled us both down to get a better look.

"It was on your porch?" I asked, glaring down at the burnt husk.

"But... but you weren't... you weren't even fucking there," Eddy stammered.

"Tell me about it." Sanders sat back in the love seat and sighed. "What if my father had found that thing?"

"We didn't say anything—" Eddy started.

"I know you didn't. You guys aren't that stupid. Throwing me under the bus would have meant you laying there with me while the tires rolled over us." That was a big analogy for a twelve-year-old, but it wasn't lost on us. "But I can't risk hanging with you guys, seeing as how Mack knows you did it. I just think it's a warning meant to tell me I need to keep my distance from you guys."

"See, I still can't wrap my head around that shit," Eddy scoffed. "He didn't see us. He couldn't *know*."

"Somebody did." Sanders looked at me and slapped his thighs. "I like you guys, believe me I do. But I'm not about to go on permanent restriction just so we can go see a movie together. Let this crap calm down, fudge off for a little bit, and maybe we'll hang when school starts."

"But..." I tried to say something, but stopped. In my heart of hearts, I knew he was right. "Come on, Eddy."

We both got up and went to the door, our heads hung low.

"I don't even think you guys should come by anymore," Sanders said, his voice sounding heavy. He didn't look upset, just sure of his decision.

"I getcha." Eddy met his eyes. "Keeping your nuts outta the fire and shit. You weren't no part of this no way."

"I'm gonna miss your double negatives, Eddy." Sanders smiled.

"See you at school, then?"

"Yep," Sanders said as he walked us out to the porch. He said nothing else, just stepped back inside and closed the door behind him.

"Who the fuck told Mack? We gotta find out who saw us," Eddy said in a hushed tone as we continued on to the Paramount.

"I don't know." I shrugged. "But I'm sure we'll find out whether we want to or not."

III

The Paramount was busier than it should have been. Usually, even during the summer, the theater was dead, mostly because everybody had seen all the movies playing there. It had been converted from a theater stage back in the early eighties, and since then, it only showed the second-run films that did well enough to garner cheaper tickets.

Eddy and I waited, hands in pockets, stepping forward slowly as the line progressed. The old-fashioned ticket booth was only ten people ahead of us, and the crowd was buzzing. Our line had grown significantly behind us. Had we arrived just a few minutes later, the seats might have been sold out. The posting above the booth displayed times for two more showings after five o'clock, but we didn't want to wait around for those.

The family in front of us caught my eye when we first stepped up behind them. The father wore a pale blue track suit, and his two daughters sported multi-colored sundresses. The girl on the right was much prettier than the other, and looked more like the father.

Our conversation with Sanders about the newest cherry bomb delivery played in my head. That was the main reason why I was looking for just about anything to keep my mind off of it. Staring at the father and two girls helped a little, but I was still distracted. Visions of Mack's cruiser door standing ajar and Eddy placing the fireworks inside shuffled through my mind. I tried to pan the camera, but it wouldn't work. I struggled to focus on our surroundings that day. Had there been someone watching? Who could it have been? Why hadn't they just hauled us in and arrested us? One thing just kept hitting me like a boxer working a punching bag, and I didn't know why.

Two extra booms.

We'd heard two *extra* booms.

"You know what?" Eddy whispered into my ear.

"Huh?"

"I look at this dude," Eddy said as low as he possibly could, pointing at the father in front of us, "and I think about Mr. Lance."

"What?" I asked, confused.

"You know, it kinda makes you look at people differently. Like is he really just out on a normal day with these two girls? Or is he trying to get in good with them to take advantage of them? Just makes me wonder, is all."

Everything slowed. The man slithered his arm over the prettier girl's back and pulled her close. A hand reached down and cupped a butt cheek, squeezing. My mouth went dry in horror as the father turned to look at me.

But he wasn't the same man.

Jude Lance looked at me with a malevolent grin spread across his face. "This stays between us, boys."

"What's wrong?" Eddy asked as I backed away. His voice sounded far away, tinny, as if through the wrong end of a megaphone.

The pretty girl's head creaked as it turned, her face melting, becoming something else right before my eyes. I must've been a sight because I heard strangers in the crowd asking what the hell was wrong with me. I bumped into someone and stumbled off to the side. A guy yelled at me to watch where I was going. I ignored him.

The pretty girl's face began to solidify, to form into a more familiar one.

Candy stared at me with blank eyes, her mouth coming open like a ventriloquist's dummy. A single tear rolled down her cheek. "Mr. Lance really seems to like me."

It all came to me quick, like a shotgun blast. My mind reeled. Visions of Candy's downcast gaze every time she talked about him. The way she'd reacted to him the night of my party. The way she looked just over an hour ago, face pale, worried, the dirty, extra-large shirt serving as a night gown, the toilet paper covering nicks on her thighs—cutting, depression, hygiene.

"Fuck!" I screamed, bellowing louder than anything, louder than everything. My mind crashed like waves against pylons. My heart cracked as it broke in my chest. I couldn't find my breath, and I really didn't care.

"Dammit, man, what's wrong with you?" Eddy asked, stepping out of line.

"Candy." I leaned against a car parked at the curb. "He's been fucking with her."

"Who?" But even as Eddy asked the question, realization played across his face. "Lance." The blood drained from his face. "Fucking shit, man. Fucking hell!" He slammed his fist into the hood of the car I was leaning on, and someone in the crowd hollered at him to get away from it.

"I... I didn't... why, Eddy?" I finally managed.

"Yeah." He groaned and shook his head, pulling at his hair as if that would help calm him down.

"We gotta do something," I said, standing straight again. My knees were weak, but I had to stand. If at no other time in my life, I absolutely had to stand. "Come on."

We ran.

IV

As scared and horrified as I was, a little relief mixed in with all the other emotions. It was terrifying, the new revelations, but it would also help matters. All I had to do was convince Candy to tell the proper authorities, and they'd lock that sadistic bastard up for the rest of his life. The plan was simple. Getting to Candy's house was the problem.

My wounded leg was burning by the time we got back to Hibiscus. I felt the blood pouring down my calf in thick strands, but it would have to wait. Crashing into Candy's front door, Eddy close behind me, I banged on it like a mad man. I was certain I looked half-crazed, and the look on Carrie Waters's face when she opened the door only cemented that fact.

"You all right, Trey?" Her eyes were frightened, but there was something else there, too.

"Is—is Candice home?" I bent over from the effort of talking. I'd just run over a mile in less than ten minutes, and my body was still trying to catch up.

"I need to talk to you. I just called your house and—"

"Is Candice here?" I yelled the question, my chest hitching from the effort.

"No," she finally said, her tone harsh. "But you and I need to talk. Eddy, you wait out here." Carrie pulled me inside, closing the door.

"I really... really need to talk to her," I gasped, still trying to catch my breath.

"What about?" Carrie asked as she pointed me to the couch.

"It's important, please," I begged, ignoring the sofa.

"I know something is going on with you and my daughter, Trey." Carrie stared at me accusingly.

"What? What are you talking about?"

"Sit down, Trey." Carrie pulled me over to the couch and pushed me down into it.

"I need to talk to—"

"Do you know what that is?" Carrie pointed to a small white stick on the coffee table. The thing had a tapered end that was brownish-yellow. Two pink lines showed brightly from a viewing window in the center of it.

"No. What's that got to—"

"It's one of my pregnancy tests. But *I* didn't take it." She picked it up and played it through her fingers.

"What does that have to do with me?"

"Did you and Candice do something the night she stayed with you in the hospital?"

"I—I don't know. What?" I remembered Candy's hand under my gown. The pleasure I'd felt. The question that went through my mind, "How does she know what's she's doing down there?"

"Nothing happened," I lied.

"Candice started her period this spring. Do you know what that is?"

"Yes," I told her, my mind struggling for answers to the crazy situation. "They taught us that in sex ed just before summer break."

"Well, then you know that means she's started producing eggs. All it takes is one time, Trey. Just one time." Carrie lowered her gaze to the pregnancy test and shook her head sadly.

"We didn't do anything," I told her. We hadn't done what she thought. There was no way. "Where is she? Why don't you ask her?"

"You kids are young, and I get that. But this…" She shook the test at me. "This is a huge responsibility for someone so young. I'm going to have to tell your parents, Trey."

"Tell them what?" I croaked, my voice cracking. "We didn't do anything!"

"This test is proof enough, Trey." She glared at me. "It's positive. Candice is pregnant."

V

I was dumbstruck, utterly speechless. Everything was too much for me to handle. My brain short-circuited, and I just sat there. I stared at that pregnancy test as if it were some alien device, something completely foreign and sinister.

"I asked your parents to come by when they got a chance. We really need to all sit down and sort this out." She looked at me, disappointment filling her face. I remained silent, awestruck. "I've been seeing Jude Lance socially. I don't know if you know that. We're getting serious, and I felt I needed to include him on this."

I snapped my head up to meet her eyes. My heart was about burst through my chest. "What?"

"He and I have been together for a little while now. Candice knows, but we haven't told anyone else because of what happened with his wife. But I had to let him know about this."

It was all coming together in my mind. Horrible visions of Mr. Lance doing things, horrible disgusting things, to Candy. His heavy body jerking on top of her. His seed driving its way through her. I stood, my breath coming in ragged gasps, my head spinning. "You did what?"

"She's over at Jude's place. I just... I just couldn't face her right now. I'm too upset. He's talking w—"

"You stupid bitch!" I ran for the door.

"Trey!" she called after me. "You can't just run away from this!"

"Call the cops! You call them right now!" I screamed at her, spittle showering from my lips. "He's the one who did it! He's the one who did this!" I ripped open the door and found Eddy looking very scared on the front porch.

"I don't understand," Carrie said from behind me. "It can't be."

"Just call the fucking cops!" I grabbed Eddy's arm and drug him down the steps. "Candy's at Lance's house. Like right now!"

"Jesus!" Eddy blared.

I said nothing else. I ran for the Lance's house with no plan, no idea what I was going to do. I just knew I had to do something.

Chapter Twelve: Of Fire Trucks and Evil

Eddy followed as I took off for Lance's porch. My mind was finally wrapping itself around everything. I had no time to feel sad or conflicted about not seeing things sooner. There was only Candy. She was all that mattered. Nothing else.

On the Lance's front porch, I twisted and pulled on the handle. I wasn't wasting any time knocking.

It was locked. I cussed loudly. Jumping down from the side of the porch, I ran around the house, past the trash bins and the air conditioning unit, to the back door. The screen door was closed and locked, but the inner door was open.

I reared back and put my leg through it with little trouble. Eddy pried the mesh away as I squeezed through the opening.

I saw Ryan first. He stood in his father's bedroom doorway, looking inside. Ryan seemed scared, but oddly fascinated. I had no idea what he was staring at, but it had stolen his attention so much that he hadn't noticed our entry.

"Get him," I told Eddy.

With that, Ryan looked back at us, a crazed expression coming onto his face. "What the fuck are—"

Eddy cut him off as he grabbed the back of Ryan's shirt and spun the kid down the hall.

Ryan screamed as he rolled down the hallway, hitting walls as he went. Stray pictures fell from the walls, crashing down around him. I left Eddy to handle him as I stepped into Jude Lance's bedroom.

I saw Candy first, her arms tied over her head to the posts of the bed. She had a sock stuffed in her mouth. Tears flooded her face. Her bloodshot eyes found me and a look of scared hope flashed in them. Jamie straddled her chest, rising and falling with her breaths. She tried to scream, but all that came out as a muffled grunt.

The fact that she was naked eluded me for a second until I saw Jude Lance.

"Just keep her still," Lance said as he played between her legs. He held something long and metal in his right hand while his left parted her opening. The slender piece of metal slid in and out of her, making slippery, wet sounds. "We'll take care of this. Don't ya worry none." His tone was comforting, playful.

"What the fuck are you doing?" I screamed, not moving, frozen to my spot.

"Trey," Lance said very nonchalantly as he turned to meet my glare. "Seems Candice here has a little problem. We're remedying that as we speak." He went back to work, sliding that steel in and out of her.

I saw the curve of the metal, the bumps where the two ends used to connect, the flat, gun-metal finish of the wire.

A clothes hanger.

He pulled the bloody end out of Candy, wiping clumps of something onto the sheets.

"Think we got it," Lance said as he rose from between her legs. "Now, to resolve another problem."

Lance rushed me, his face calm and frightening. We crashed back against the wall of the hallway. He didn't say a word as he wrapped his hands around my throat and squeezed. The man wasn't much taller than I was, but he outweighed me by at least a hundred pounds. I instantly started to see stars. I did the only thing I could think of.

I kneed him in the balls.

The wind from his lungs covered my face as the air rushed from him. His grasp loosened, and I drove my knee once more into his crotch, then again. He stumbled back and bent over to grab at his balls. I kicked as hard as I could, and his nose disappeared behind sheets of red.

Mr. Lance went down hard.

I found Eddy pounding Ryan in the living room. Running over to him, I snatched him off the kid, trying to speak through a sore larynx. "Call... an ambulance... quick."

Eddy nodded, kicking Ryan in the ribs one more time before moving for the phone in the kitchen. I decided to unlock the front door for the authorities, but when I turned my back to the hallway, something crashed into me.

I flailed my arms, screaming as I went down. My hands sought purchase on the rows of shelving that held the die-cast replicas Lance was so fond of, tearing them from the wall.

Everything came crashing down, the cars, me, and Mr. Lance on my back. I felt myself come up almost immediately, spinning over, then a pressure on my chest. Mr. Lance straddled me. He laughed as he punched me in the throat. He pulled it at the last minute, for whatever reason, and it only grazed me.

Grabbing me by the shoulders, he raised me up and slammed me back to the ground. The wind kicked from me, but I had no trouble drawing another breath. He did it again and again until my vision started to spin.

My roaming hand found something. It was cold against the palm of my hand. And very solid. All I could think about was surviving. Whatever the hell I held would have to be a good enough weapon.

Blood from Lance's shattered nasal passages rained down onto my chest and chin as he leaned in to choke me again. His icy fingers made their way around my throat.

I saw a flash of red as I quickly brought up my hand, and the object connected with Mr. Lance's temple. His eyes rolled back in his head. He rolled off of me. Limp. Done. Anger, horror, and a need for retribution filled me. I pushed myself up on my elbows and looked at the thing in my hand.

It was Mr. Lance's cast iron replica of a fire truck. I raised it up over my head as far as it would go, bringing it down on his forehead with a deafening crack. There was blood, lots of it, as his brow opened in a ragged gash. I brought the truck down again and split his left cheek open just under his eye. Officer Mack's face flashed into my head, the torn flesh reminding me of that scar of his, and my anger flared even more.

I felt someone pulling me away. I thrashed wildly and screamed, all semblance of sanity leaving me. I heard Eddy trying to calm me down, heard him trying to rein in my demons.

I choked on my own tears and retched onto the floor beside Ryan's trembling form. The stuff that came out of me was thick and green. My eyes burned as I voided my stomach all over the floor. My body twitched and bucked. I felt Eddy's hand on my back.

I wailed as I retched.

Eddy said, "It's all right. Everything's going to be all right. Somebody's coming, and it's all going to be okay."

But he was wrong. Nothing would ever be all right again. Nothing could ever be okay. Not anymore. The world had changed. It had become a dark place full of evil and monsters and terrible things. And the worst part was that I had no control over any of it.

Chapter Thirteen: Aftermath

I remember going down the hallway, leaning against the wall as I walked. I went to the bed where Candy lay, still bound. Jamie cowered in the corner, crying, fear, and confusion in his eyes. He blubbered something about "bubberflies."

Candy's eyes rolled in her head. Her face was pale and slick with sweat. I untied the stereo cords that bound her, and her hands just fell limply to her sides. I pulled the sock from her mouth.

I crawled into the bed next to her. I held her limp form against myself, crying, apologizing, begging her to forgive me.

She never said a word.

Everything else happened in quick flashes. Carrie came in, screaming. She pushed me away, but I didn't want to go. I *couldn't* let Candy go.

Carrie tore me from her daughter as she scooped her damaged baby into her arms.

I just lay there, not thinking, not living, just existing.

The ambulance came first, then the cops. There were questions I couldn't answer. Spots I couldn't fill in. There were assurances that everything was over. I could answer later. I could tell my story later.

Later.

I was checked over in the back of a waiting ambulance. They even bandaged my leg again. I think I thanked them, but I can't be sure. Abstract bullshit, you know.

Lance survived, but he was left with one hell of a face. I take some comfort in the fact that every time he would look at himself in the mirror, for the rest of his life, he would think about me and relive what I did to him. Everybody assured me he was going to spend a very long time in jail once everything was said and done. That bit didn't comfort me. I wanted him dead. But I had failed in my chance.

Candy made it through, as well. I went to see her in the hospital every day over the following week. She never spoke, never even acknowledged my presence. She just lay there, glassy-eyed, staring off into a distant world. It broke my heart. Ripped it from my very chest. Once again, I had failed.

Finally, on my last visit, I made my case. As poorly as it came off, it was heartfelt. I begged her to forgive me. Told her I loved her. But when I leaned in to kiss her on the cheek, she slapped me across the cheek and began to scream. She kicked, bucked, and thrashed until the nurses came in to sedate her. They asked me what I did. I told them I didn't do anything.

The truth was I hadn't done enough. I had been too late.

The last time I saw Candy was that day, the day she hit me as though I were Mr. Lance attacking her again. I could see it in her eyes. That fiery hatred. That cold fear.

Candy and Carrie disappeared once Candy was well enough to travel. Carrie abandoned their home and just left, leaving everything behind. No one knew where they went. I just hoped it was to a special place where Candy could heal. Could forget. A land of wonders and enchantment where there were no fire trucks or clothes hangers.

Interlude 5: Closure

I have buried Romo and burned the remains. I have dealt with the memory of Jude Lance and have cast it into the void. They are gone, forgotten now. No longer will they haunt me.

Now for the final ghost.

Eddy is crying, silent and forlorn. He knows the end is here. He sits there, nodding as if to strengthen me, to give me that final confidence I will need to tell his story. This all began with his memory. And now, it will end with it.

We've taken this journey to expel the terrors that have formed me as a man. The fears have been vanquished, but the scars remain. The final scar is not mine. Never has been. Eddy sacrificed for me. Now I must return the favor.

The events you've witnessed here, the blood, the tears, my very soul played out before you, have been to prepare you for what is to come. If those things hadn't happened, if I hadn't lived through those things, been those things, the ending of this story would have been different.

Eddy gave me the courage to deal with what was to come. He was a constant, my cherished constant. That summer was our only time together, but it felt like forever. Then again, it didn't feel like enough. I loved that boy. You've heard the term, 'brother I've never had,' but it's never been more correct. If Candy was my heart and soul, Eddy was my strength.

You could argue that if I had never met Eddy, if those cherry bombs had never been planted, none of this would have happened to me. I say you're wrong. Dead wrong. He was my saving grace. Not my damnation. For if it weren't for him, Mack Larson would still be an officer of the law, and no one would have ever dealt with him.

Here we are, old friend.

The final mile...

Chapter Fourteen: Vigil

I

August 20th, 1992

Eddy and I spent a great deal of time together over the next four weeks, mostly playing video games and tossing the ball around, but we were also figuring out who we were going to be, the men we were to become. Eddy's father had signed him up for a metalworking class the school system offered as a summer program. I took a class as well, a creative writing course. Sanders signed up for it, too, but we still weren't talking. Every now and then, he'd look my direction, a wan smile on his face, and I'd return it before we both resumed our studies. I missed him, and by the looks of it, he felt the same way. It just wasn't the right time, and I knew it.

After the incident with Mr. Lance, The End had taken a look at itself and not liked what it had seen. Emily Harper became a symbol, something the town could get right. A bastion of hope after a tragedy. They only needed to find her.

The candlelight vigil for Emily Harper was on a Sunday, a week before school started up again. I decided to go, not because of Emily, but because I needed some time to mourn Candy. Sure, she wasn't dead, but she was as close to dead as she would get for me. I had ignored my feelings of loss for an entire month. It was time to grieve.

Eddy came with my parents and me. His folks had other things to do. A bottle of whiskey and a backache for his dad; a night of laughter for his mom as *Comic Relief '92* would be playing for the entire length of the vigil. They didn't know Emily Harper, so it wasn't as if they were supposed to go. Eddy only came along because he knew why I was going. Plain and simple.

The End was comprised of three separate sections. On one end was the Westerns. The main body of the town held the Paramount, the laundromat, Rifle Park, and various other shops and stores, including Peaton's Grocery. The third section contained the fairgrounds, nothing more than a vacant lot with one hundred acres of deforested land. Back in the sixties, the place was a theater venue and actually served as the original Paramount location. It had been a drive-in during that incarnation. My parents told me that was where they'd first met while on a double date, centuries ago before the dinosaurs. The piece of land was owned by Waverly Fairchild, so some called it Fairchild Farm, even though there was no farm, and Waverly hadn't lived there in over a decade. Waverly owned a good deal of Bay's End and was the one who had started the bonfires back in the late seventies. After contracting a carnival out of Canada somewhere, The End started holding yearly fairs and festivals, funded by Waverly Fairchild, during the autumn months. I don't know whatever happened to Waverly, but the carnival still comes around every October and stays until the weekend before Thanksgiving.

When Dad pulled the station wagon into the makeshift parking lot of the fairgrounds, I saw Jenna Wales coming around the side of a little

Dodge pickup. I waved as I got out of the car. She saw me, I was certain, but she didn't wave back. I didn't think much of it at the time, just figuring she was in a bad mood.

Old Hap Carringer was handing out candles with little paper circles attached to the bottoms to protect our hands from the dripping wax. He looked ancient. I couldn't help but wonder just how old the man was. "Trey Franklin, as I live and breathe," he rasped as we approached. Years of smoking Camel non-filters had done a number on his vocal chords. He was smoking one then, too. It was tucked between two yellowed fingers, tendrils of smoke snaking through the air. "Look at'cha! You done gone and grow'd up on this old man!"

"Hello, Chief." I offered him a forced smile.

"Tough times make tough people, Trey." Hap winked, a sadness to his face. "You did good by that girl. So's I heard it told. Jude Lance is still in ICU." He laughed and coughed, a fit that took some time to go away. "Damn cigarettes. You don't get to smokin', you hear me, boy?"

"Yes, Chief." I nodded as Dad patted my scruffy head. My hair was just starting to fill in again, something for which I was grateful.

"Trust me," Dad told him. "He won't. Not if we have anything to say about it."

"You're a local hero, yourself, Danny." Hap tipped his Boston Red Sox hat toward my father. "Got that werewolf a silver bullet luncheon, dint'cha?"

"Was a little late, Hap." Dad sighed. "Not a hero in my eyes."

"Real heroes never are in their *own* eyes. Don't lessen the fact, though. Damn pooch shoulda been put down ages ago. Nuttin' but trouble that half-breed was. All the rage upstate, you know, them wolf mixes."

"Remind me never to go up north," Eddy finally spoke up.

"Ahoy!" Hap laughed himself into another coughing fit. "Boy's, ahem, got a sense of humor! Whose kid are you?"

"Eddy Treemont, sir. My dad's the new—"

"Night sweep o'er to the school. Law's yes, I know of him. Never met the man, but good people, so's Sulan Sanderson tells. Hard worker. Where is he tonight?"

"It's that hard work that has him laid up with a bad back," Eddy said. "Bad nerves and... stuff." I knew Eddy wanted to say "and shit," but he caught himself just in time.

"Bad thing a messed-up back is. Laid up, you say?"

"He won't miss any work. My old man works whether he hurts or not," Eddy said proudly. "Just didn't want to stand outside all night and pay for it in the morning."

"Fart smeller." Hap feigned shock and laughed. It sounded far too forced. "I mean, smart feller." He winked at Eddy.

I missed Hap for that reason. The man was always riding around town in his brown cruiser—the only one in town that was that color, and they'd let him keep it even after retirement—giving people a helping hand and passing sweet stuff out to the kids on the block. He seemed an all-around good man. Stoic and hard as nails. Yet, nice and soft like a teddy bear. It was a shame to see him all wrinkled and gray, showing his true years.

I followed my parents through the crowd with Eddy at my side. A pretty teenage girl was lighting candles with a Bic lighter as people passed. I held out mine, and she did the honors. Her smile reminded me of Candy, and I had to swallow a lump the size of Texas before walking on.

I had to keep reminding myself why I was there. The night was for Emily Harper, but my heart was with Candy. I saw her here and there, milling through the crowd. I knew it wasn't really her, but it hurt all the same.

They had a stage set up in the middle of the field. Towers of speakers lay to each side of the oval platform. Doug Harper, Emily's father and the owner of Harper's Fine Goods, stood on the stage, talking with a man I didn't know.

My heart sank when Doug stepped to the side, and I recognized Mack Larson. He was smiling, his scar twitching in the stadium lights that surrounded Fairchild Farm. Eddy elbowed me and pointed to the stage. I nodded. I was sure neither one of us looked very happy.

Once we reached a decent spot, Dad stopped. We were a good twenty yards from the stage, but we weren't getting any closer. Half of Bay's End must have been in attendance. It reminded me of Hap's retirement party, only thicker.

We stood and waited while more people filtered in. You would have thought the girl was a town celebrity the way folks gathered for the event. I thought people just wanted something to do. The End wasn't exactly the most booming of towns. That kind of social gathering brought

315

people out of the woodwork like poisoned roaches.

About ten minutes after we arrived, the microphone on the stage squealed as it was turned on. Mack Larson, of all people, stepped forward.

"Hello, everybody." Mack cleared his throat and smiled. "First and foremost, I would like to thank Chaz. Where are you, Chaz? There you go. Thanks to Chaz for letting us borrow the sound equipment from his after-hours joint over in Chestnut." Mack stepped back to clap, and the crowd gave a resounding applause. "Good guy, that Chaz is. I also need to thank my predecessor, Hap Carringer." Another pause for applause, louder than the last one. "For helping to put all this together. Hap came out of pocket for the candles and everything, so make sure to thank him when you see him on your way out. But this isn't why we are here. There is a more upsetting reason for all of us to be gathered tonight. That reason is Emily Harper."

The crowd grew quiet as they watched Doug Harper approach the microphone, waiting for his introduction.

"Doug Harper has been worried sick since Emily first disappeared over a month ago. We're gathered here tonight to offer him our support. He would like to say a few words before we continue. Doug?"

There was no applause as Doug moved for the microphone, no roars of welcome. Only sad, depressing silence. It was as if they'd already found Emily dead and had just buried her. The vigil had taken on the tone of a funeral.

"Hello, my fellow members of Bay's End." Doug swallowed and his throat clicked. "I'm here tonight to beg for your help. I plead with you, if you have any information..." He stopped for a minute, his fist coming to his mouth. He bit down on a knuckle, trying his best to hold back a torrent of emotions that surely threatened to overcome him. "...any information on the whereabouts of my daughter, please come forward. If you know where she might have gone, if you've seen her, or seen someone with her, please just tell someone. It doesn't have to be me. It can be anyone, anywhere. Just please, please, tell *someone*."

My heart sank. I saw Emily Harper's smiling face from the picture hanging in the window of Harper's Fine Goods. I saw her crying, begging for a modicum of leniency from the very man who stood next to her worrying father. I saw

Eddy putting the cherry bombs in the front seat of Mack's cruiser. Saw the trees rush by as the three of us fled into Rifle Park, laughing like a bunch of vigilantes, as if we'd won a small battle in an ever-expanding war.

I heard the explosions:

Boom! Boom! Boom! Boom! Boom! Boom!

I flinched.

Four cherry bombs, but six explosions. Something was there in that information, but I couldn't put the pieces together. It was right there. So close. Yet, still so far away. For better or for worse, I knew right then and there, I had to tell someone what we'd done. I looked at Eddy and automatically knew he was thinking the same thing.

"You sure?" he whispered in my ear.

"Not a doubt in my mind."

II

I told Mom and Dad we were going to walk around for a while, and they didn't protest. After their perfunctory 'be careful,' we left to find Jenna Wales. Though the entire township seemed to be there that evening, she wasn't that hard to find. There was an old wooden fence that surrounded the Fairchild Farm, and it mostly served to keep kids out during the carnival days, but Jenna was using it as a leaning post. She was watching the proceedings on the stage—Mack Larson going over Emily Harper's last known whereabouts—until she caught sight of us coming out of the crowd. She didn't smile, didn't wave, just waited silently as we approached.

"Hey, Jenna," I said, walking up to her. "You got a minute?"

"For?"

"Did I, uh, do something?" I was starting to rethink my idea of talking to her.

"Just a shitty night, Trey. Sorry." She crossed her arms over her chest and tossed her head back, her blond hair blowing in the night's breeze.

"Anything *you* wanna talk about?" We had come to spill our guts, not play therapist, but she looked like she needed someone to talk to.

"It's just... never mind." She cussed under her breath and stomped her foot into the dirt. "I'm sorry about Candice, boys. I just wish there was something I could've done."

"It wasn't your fault, Jen," Eddy said. He didn't know the woman from Adam, but he could see, just as I could, that she needed some reassurance.

She pointed at Mack on the stage, "He let that shit go too far. He came back to the office that night after talking to you, Trey, complaining about you causing trouble and some shit about a wild goose chase. I was the only one there, the only fucking person who heard him say it, so it's my word against his. Now he's not going to see any repercussions for letting what happened to Candice occur. He's still a fucking hero in this screwed-up town's eyes, and I can't live with that shit. Sorry about my language."

"Pardon your French, huh?" Eddy scoffed.

"You've heard him say that?"

"Plenty," I answered. "We don't have the best history with Mack. You know that."

"Fucking asshole," Eddy growled as he pushed his wire rims up his nose.

"You can say that again." Jenna laughed, loosening up a little. I could tell the way the hard edges of her shoulders softened as she exhaled that she was cooling off. I didn't know if I wanted her cool, though.

"You may not want to hear this," I said. "But I kinda didn't tell you the whole story."

"About what?"

"Emily Harper."

"And?" Her face changed. "You two didn't—"

"Fuck, no," Eddy blurted. "We didn't have anything to do with her vanishing act."

"Well, not fully responsible, anyway," I added.

"What do you mean, 'not fully responsible?' Listen, you two, spill your guts, or this conversation is over. Like right now. You understand me?" A fire lit in her eyes. I'd never been scared of her until that moment, so the next line just fell out of my mouth.

"We put the cherry bombs in Mack's car the day Emily disappeared." I said it so fast I might as well have been rapping. It just spilled forth, untethered, out into the night like verbal defecation.

I was surprised to see the lack of surprise on her face. "I kinda figured that. I assumed it was the reason he was watching you kids like a hawk. Him having everyone keep an eye on you and what not started the night after he pulled into the parking lot with a roasted driver's seat. But what does that have to do with the Harper girl?"

"Mack had her pulled over when we did it. That's how we got them in there. Emily was begging for a break, not wanting to get a ticket. Mack was filling out his booklet like he wasn't going to let her slide. Eddy and I snuck up and planted them—"

"I planted them. You're not taking the fall, buddy. Sorry."

"But I looked out. I watched while you did it. Candy was there, too. We took off into the woods."

"And left Mack there with Emily Harper?"

"Yeah." Eddy nodded. "He was the last one to see her. We saw her missing poster a couple days later."

"We didn't know what to do. We were just being a bunch of stupid kids. We didn't want any of this to happen." I let my emotions take over and started to bawl like a little baby. "Now, she's missing, and Candy's gone, and Sanders is all fucked up over us, and I don't—"

Jenna slapped me. I stumbled back, but Eddy caught me before I hit the ground.

"What...?"

"Why didn't you tell me?" she hissed. "Her father is up there, begging for some help from this haphazard fucking community, standing up there with the last man who saw his daughter alive, and you two knew he was involved? What the...? Oh shit, never mind!" She spun around and slugged the wooden paneling of the fence. She actually managed to crack the wood.

"I'm sorry." I sucked some stray snot up my nose. "We're trying to make this right. I promise we'll make this right."

"Kinda late for that," Jenna said, calming a bit. "You didn't see what happened to Emily?"

"No." Eddy's voice cracked. "We swear."

"So what happened to her?" It was a rhetorical question, and we knew it.

"Wha—what do we do now?" I stammered. I was managing to control myself, but the tears were still coming.

"I don't know. Really." She ran a hand through her hair. "I guess we won't know unless we find her. She could be anywhere. That's why we never got a search party together. It's not like we found a car ditched somewhere, or any sign of foul play at her home."

My cheek burned like fire, but I supposed I deserved it. "We gotta do something."

"I know. Just give me a minute to think." Jenna leaned back against the fence and sucked in a long deep breath. "Where would you go if you didn't want anyone to find you?"

Eddy shrugged. "The Westerns?"

Jenna grabbed Eddy by the front of his shirt. "You're fucking brilliant, kid!"

"What'd I do?"

"Yeah," I whispered, starting to see what she was getting at. "If you want to go somewhere and not be bothered, you go to the Westerns. You want to hide something? You go to the Westerns. Mack knows that. He knows—"

"—that you kids wouldn't go back there if you wanted to!" Jenna finished. "No one would. He keeps that place on lockdown. It was one of his orders. 'You see those kids around the Westerns, and you call me, personally.' I could kiss you, Eddy!"

"Don't let me stop you." Eddy flashed his bucks.

"So, what do we do now?" I asked.

Jenna let go of Eddy's shirt and looked over at me. "We go looking for her."

"And what happens when we find her?"

"We call someone who will listen. State police are only a phone call away, but they won't come unless we have some evidence. So, we head out there and see what we can find."

"We?" Eddy asked, looking shocked.

"I'm not letting you boys out of my goddamn sight. If Mack thinks for even a moment that you guys told me, we won't have a chance of finding Emily." She frowned. "If we find her at all."

"When are we doing this?" I asked.

"No time like the present," Jenna said.

"Tonight?" Eddy blurted.

"You got something else to do?" Jenna gave us a quizzical stare.

We both looked at each other, shrugged, and shook our heads.

"What about my parents?" I asked.

"I hate to say this because I'd hate for your Mom to worry, but she'll understand once we bring her up to speed. She's going to be pissed at you enough when she finds out about the cherry bombs, don't ya think?"

"She's got a point." Eddy laughed, stopping almost as soon as he began. I guess he realized it wasn't all that funny.

"Let's go, kiddos," Jenna said.

Chapter Fifteen: The Westerns

I

Just before the sun went down, I'd seen the beginning of a summer storm brewing in the north, but I hadn't expected it to arrive so soon. The first drops of rain began to pelt the windows of Jenna's Explorer as we drove through the abandoned streets of Bay's End. The windshield wipers made a hollow *Snap-Click, Snap-Click* as they danced before my eyes.

Jenna took a right off of Main Street where it forked into Juniper. It wasn't long before lightning in the distance highlighted the Dark

Room. The tall stone structure seemed to bear down on us as we approached. I shivered, but when Jenna looked my way, I pretended the air coming out of the vents caused it.

She pulled the Explorer to the side of the road and turned off the engine. Reaching over my lap, she popped open the glove box, revealing a shiny silver handgun like the one detectives used in those old crime dramas. I knew it was a revolver from watching *Magnum P.I.* with my dad.

Jenna stuffed the gun in the waist of her jeans. She swung out of the car, then bent back inside, pulling a police issue Maglite from under her driver's seat. She clicked it on, and the beam washed over my face, blinding me for a second.

"Sorry 'bout that." She smiled grimly and turned off the torch. "You guys coming?"

It was an unneeded question, as Eddy already had his door open and was climbing out.

"This place never does cease to give me the chills," Jenna said as she clicked the button on the flashlight and played it across the buildings in the distance. I didn't know what was lowest on my to-do list: Finding Emily Harper, or going in *there* to find her.

God, please don't let Emily be in The Dark Room, I prayed silently as we approached the gate.

Jenna's light flitted over the chain-link fence that barred our entrance, raindrops falling in the beam. I wiped the wet from my head. My hand ran over my bandage, and I grimaced. "My dressing. Shit." I wiped the rainwater off on my pants.

"There's a hoodie in the backseat. Go back and grab it," Jenna said, flipping her flashlight in the direction of the SUV.

Running back to the truck, I popped open the rear passenger door. A blue zip-up sweater was laying over the backseat. I slipped it on and tossed the hood over my head to protect the back of my neck. Jogging back, I joined them at the gate.

"He replaced the chain." Eddy pointed. The new stainless steel link shined within the torch's beam. "The last one was rusted, wasn't it?"

"Yeah." I shivered. Just that little time under the rain had frozen me to my core.

"That's heavy link and a massive lock. I have bolt cutters in the hatch by the tire well, but they won't even begin to cut that," Jenna said. "I guess it's over we go."

Eddy sighed and began to climb the fence.

I had a fleeting worry about my leg, but ignored it. I dug my sneakers into the link and pulled myself up beside Eddy. I landed hard on the other side, fresh mud spilling up and over my Nikes. Jenna tossed the flashlight over to us, and Eddy caught it. The gun was handed through the gap near the hinged posts. Jenna climbed over, making it look like a flawless effort.

"Where'd you learn how to climb a damn fence?" Eddy asked in awe.

"I was a kid not too long ago, buster." She grinned in the glow of the torch. "Ask Trey. I'm only about ten years older than you."

"That might as well be a hundred where I'm concerned," Eddy added dryly.

"Eat me." Jenna smiled mockingly.

"Anytime… anywhere."

"Guys!" I growled. "You do remember why we're here?" Did I really have to play adult in this situation? I just couldn't believe it.

"Sorry." Eddy shrugged. He handed the gun back to Jenna, and I kept the flashlight.

"Shall we?" Jenna asked.

"Lead the way, oh, captain, my captain!" Eddy saluted.

II

I was kind of hoping that it would be as easy as following tire tracks or footprints or something like that, but the rain made it impossible. Even if it hadn't been storming, it was dark. Too damn dark. And aside from the small, thin beam of the flashlight, we were blind.

Since the South Building was the biggest place on the property, we decided to start there.

"Feels like forever since we were last out here," Eddy said, breaking the silence that had hovered over us while we walked.

"Not long enough." I laughed nervously.

"And what was it I said last time we were here? Something about growing a pair. How's that working out for you?"

"I'm not in the mood, Eddy."

"Understood," he said, sounding apologetic enough.

"You two sound like you've known each other forever," Jenna observed.

"Something like that," I grumbled.

The first time we were there together, Eddy hadn't found an entrance to South Building. We hadn't had a flashlight, either. The large wooden double doors were painted the same color as the peeling red paint of the rest of the building. Its hinges were set inside the wood, painted over, almost invisible. No wonder we hadn't found it. We'd found the doors on the left side of the building strictly by accident. What had caught Jenna's attention was the rainwater running underneath the doors from somewhere inside.

She laid her hand on the rusty handle and pulled. The door squealed, but gave way easy enough. A musty, dank odor filled our lungs. Unfortunately, the smell reminded me of death. I'd found a decaying raccoon under the house the previous winter while helping Dad fix a busted pipe that had frozen and broken. South Building smelled like that, if not worse.

Jenna lit the way as we stepped inside.

The floors were smooth concrete. They were slippery where mold had grown over the years. Rainwater came from a hole in the roof about fifty feet above us, splashing down onto the stone floor. Jenna worked the flashlight across the expanse. The chamber looked to be as long as a football field and as wide as an aircraft hangar. The torch flipped from left to right, dying just thirty yards ahead in the blackness. We skirted the waterfall coming from the hole overhead and moved deeper into South Building.

"This place is huge," Eddy whispered.

"And empty." Jenna sighed.

The walls that seemed to go on forever in the dark soon came to an end at the far wall. We'd walked the entire expanse of the building without seeing so much as a pile of dirt in a corner. For as long as the place had been left dormant to rot away, forgotten by the world, it was awfully clean. I could only imagine the time and effort that had been taken when the logging company moved out of there. They must've scrubbed the place down to the concrete before they left.

"What's that?" Eddy pointed at the wall.

A billboard hung lopsided on the back wall. Yellowed papers clung to it, held up by brass thumbtacks. We walked over and scanned the documents.

Jenna read aloud the first one in the top left corner. "Notice. This building is set for closure. All production is to cease and desist until further work orders are given." She shined the torch over to the next one, and I took over.

"Carringer and Sons Logging will be going out of business this April twentieth, nineteen..." I leaned in to read it better, peeling the dog-eared corner away so I could finish it. "... seventy-one. Please have your lockers cleared and your time cards filled out seven days prior to termination of production. Failure to do so could result in lost wages."

"Carringer?" Jenna said, furrowing her brow in the light of the torch. "Chief's family owns this place?"

"I didn't know that," I said.

"Neither does anyone else," Jenna added. "I can promise you that."

"So, why would anyone cover up that Hap's family owned this place?" I asked.

"Beats me." The flashlight bobbed over to the final notice and Jenna read it. "Enacted April twenty-second. That's two days after they closed. All personnel caught on site will be prosecuted for trespassing. The basement floors of South Building and the Carringer Cummings building—"

"Basements?" Eddy mumbled.

"Shush," I hissed.

Jenna continued, unabated by Eddy's interruption. "... will be sealed off. Anyone with any personal items in these areas should consider them forfeit after said date. Yours, Harold Carringer."

"Wait. You're telling me Hap himself signed this?" I leaned in to look at the scribbled signature. Just under it, in bold type, was his full name: Harold Mackenzie Carringer. "Mackenzie?" I laughed. "Gotta love those old names. Only Mackenzies around nowadays are girls."

"I don't know." Eddy shrugged. "I knew a dude back in Toledo named Mackenzie. Nice kid."

"Nice kid?" I chuckled. "Doesn't sound like the Eddy I know."

"How did the chief of police come to own a logging company?" Jenna asked. "Just doesn't make sense."

"I'm more interested in these basements," Eddy stated, flashing his bucks.

"It says they were sealed over two decades ago, dude," I said.

"Yeah. And? Doesn't mean someone didn't *unseal* them."

"He's got a point. What better place to hide something?" Jenna asked.

"We don't even know where these sealed entrances are," I pointed out.

"That's why we're here, right?" Eddy said.

I sighed. "Do you have to keep reminding me?"

"Obviously, I do. Now, come on."

"Check the floors closer this time. We coulda missed something." Jenna took the lead, playing the beam across the concrete.

The light shifted subtly as it moved along a crease in the floor about as wide as a pencil. If we hadn't had the flashlight, we would have walked right over it. The steel grate was the same color as the concrete and easily mistaken for another part of the floor. Jenna trained the beam on the latch. A round loop had been welded into the bracket, making opening it look impossible. Upon further inspection, I saw that the metal around the rim had been pried open, probably with a crowbar.

"Bingo," Jenna breathed.

"Help me out," Eddy said as he bent over and tucked the tips of his fingers into the crease of the metal. I crouched and shoved my fingers into the slit. Together, we lifted the heavy door while Jenna held the flashlight.

The smell of rot and decay hit us like a tangible thing. Eddy and I slung the metal door up and over. The sound of it ringing off the floor echoed powerfully. We all clapped our hands to our ears until the noise finally faded away.

"Shit, that was loud!" Eddy yelled.

"Is that a ladder?" Jenna asked, shining the light into the tunnel below.

"Looks like it." I saw the iron rungs in the beam. The thing looked as rusted out as everything else we had come across, but completely intact.

Jenna smiled. "Please, you first."

III

The rusted iron dug into my palms as I descended the ladder. I prayed that a stray barb wouldn't break my skin. The last thing I needed was lead poisoning. I could imagine myself with lockjaw, trying to mumble an excuse to my parents about why I was such a moron. I counted each rung as I went down, something I had never done before, but wanting to know just how deep I was going was high on my list of things to figure out. My foot suddenly hit bottom, and I almost fell backward into the darkness. My damp Nikes squeaked on the dry floor.

"Catch!" Jenna hollered down just before a cylinder of light came spinning toward me. I caught it without a problem, but I would have liked a little advanced warning.

"Just shine that thing up here while we come down," Eddy yelled.

The air down there was foul, but fresh air was coming from somewhere. I could feel a light breeze on my face. I stood with the beam of the flashlight shining upward as Eddy came down, followed shortly by Jenna. Eddy's rubber soles made the same squeak on the ground as mine had. Once Jenna was safe, I shined the light over our new environment.

The walls were concrete, but the ground was black asphalt, tarry with a little give to it. Road asphalt doesn't do well in wet environs, so I wasn't surprised to see random weeds and crabgrass growing here and there through cracks.

"Looks like the underground railroad," Eddy said.

"And how would you know what an underground railroad looked like?" I asked, laughing.

"Well, it's underground." He pointed to a line of metal in the middle of the odd-looking subterranean road. "And it has a rail."

I didn't bother telling Eddy the Underground Railroad had actually been a system for smuggling runaway slaves away from the South and into the North, not a locomotive line. I didn't have time to explain Harriet Tubman, either.

"This just keeps getting stranger and stranger." Jenna sighed. "Onward, I s'pose."

If I had my bearings correct, we were heading toward the Green House. We followed the single rail until the tunnel began to narrow into a passageway no wider than Jenna. I led Eddy and her with the torch's beam to the ground, making sure I didn't suddenly stumble over some great chasm to my death. There was no telling how far down we were. I'd counted twenty-four rungs on the ladder, but by the grade of the passageway, we were moving further south. Not South Pole south. Hell south.

Eventually, we came to a wider section of the tunnel. It was circular, a large open expanse the size of South Building at least. Two more archways were on the wall to our left and directly ahead. The one on the left, I assumed, would lead us to the Dark Room. The one on the right? I didn't know.

In the dead center of the chamber was a sight that stopped my heart. I heard Eddy gasp and Jenna stop breathing at the exact same time.

"Is that what I think it is?" Jenna whispered.

"Sure as hell looks that way." I shined the flashlight beam over the blue sedan, making sure to find the small letters on the back of it.

A Honda Civic. A blue one.

"Emily," was all I could manage.

IV

We approached the car with caution, not knowing what, or who, we would find inside once we got there.

The driver's side window was rolled down. I shined the flashlight inside, and the smell hit me about the same time the sight did. There was blood. Lots of blood. More blood than I'd ever seen in my life. It was congealed in the passenger seat, a black puddle on white upholstery. Chunks and meaty fragments littered the floorboards and dash. The passenger side window looked like some abstract splatter painting, glinting brown in the beam of the torch.

Jenna exhaled sharply. "Holy shit."

"Smells like a slaughterhouse in there." Eddy pinched his nose.

"Looks like we found out what happened to Emily Harper," Jenna whispered, her voice sounding hollow in the round chamber.

"So where is she?" I asked.

"Good question," Jenna answered.

I used my shirt to pull open the driver's side door. The only place we couldn't see was the trunk. I leaned into the well and hunted for the release. The white car emblem with an open trunk stared back at me from beside the clutch. Pulling the lever, I heard the *plunk* of the hatch as it popped open. The three of us rounded the back of the car, and I hesitantly shined the flashlight into the holding compartment.

Emily Harper, mouth frozen open, stared up at us through glazed-over cataracts. The first bullet had entered just above her right eye; the second looked to have traveled through her nose, or what was left of it. Her blond hair was strewn in a bloody, strawberry halo, stiff with hardened blood. Ragged bits of scalp jutted up from behind her head. Gone was the smiling girl from the missing poster. Vanished was the sobbing girl who had been begging to get out of a ticket. All that was left was an empty shell. Emily Harper was gone. Like our burnt-out cherry bombs, a discarded husk of what once was.

"He killed her." Eddy shook his head. "That crazy fucker blew out her goddamn brains."

"Why?" I asked.

"Who the fuck knows?" All the color had left Jenna's face. "My God, her father."

"What do we do now?" Eddy asked.

"We call the state police, like I said. We make a statement, and we get them—"

I saw the flashes before I heard the shots. Sound plays tricks on you in a closed environment. Jenna was standing next to Eddy, illuminated in the flashlight's beam. The next second, she wasn't there. Cut off in mid-sentence.

I think I screamed, but I can't really remember. The flashes had come from mystery door number one, the archway opposite the way we'd come in. I spun on my heels and found the spot where I'd seen the bursts. I heard the soft *clop, clop, clop* of hard soles on asphalt.

Mack Larson walked into the beam of the flashlight.

I heard a sound coming to the surface. A light "tsk tsk tsk" filled the chamber, the sound of a parent disappointed in a child.

"The stupid bitch knew better than to cross me." Mack glared at me over the top of his handgun. The barrel was still smoking. I squinted as he turned on his flashlight. "My, my, my, what a fucked-up sitch-ee-ation we done got ourselves into right here! Hooey!"

I didn't dare take my eyes off him, but the urge to check on Jenna was far too great. Eddy had disappeared along the side of the sedan, and he was waving me over. I ducked down and let my back go flush with its fender. We cowered there, side by side. I didn't know who was breathing heavier, me or him.

"You didn't have to shoot her, asshole!" Eddy finally screamed.

"'Course I did, boys. Can't let word get out that I'm not a good, upstanding peacekeeper. What would my father think of me? Eh?" Mack called, "And you can play hide and go seek all you want. But it's going to end up just like it did with Ryan and Jamie. No good at all with a wicked surprise ending!"

I shined the flashlight over the ground until I found Jenna's legs. I slowly trailed it up until I reached her stomach. Blood was pooling there, darkening her white shirt, but her chest rose and fell. She was alive. At least for the moment.

Scanning further up, I found the barrel of a gun pointed in our direction. Jenna had the thing hanging loose in her palm, but I about shit myself when I saw it. Drawing the light to her face, I watched far too much blood spill from her mouth, and she hacked it onto the asphalt.

She blinked her eyes at me, pleading, begging me to do something. With a flick of her wrist, the revolver skated across the blacktop toward Eddy. He scooped it up in one fluid motion as if he'd been trained to do it. Jenna's eyes shot toward Mack's direction, then to us, back and forth. She brought her index finger up and pointed to him. Then, laying it against her temple, she jerked her thumb as if blowing her brains out.

"Don't worry," Eddy whispered. "I fully intend it." Then to me, he said, "Cut the light, Trey."

Mack called, "Here piggy, piggy, piggy! Come out, come out, wherever you are!"

Chapter Sixteen: In The Dark

Mack clicked off his own flashlight, and we were thrust into the black. It was dark, cave dark, and if it wasn't for the car at my back, I would have had no idea which direction I was facing. I felt a soft tug on my shirt as Eddy pulled at me. I heard him sliding around and wished he would just hold still.

"Dow—" Eddy hissed. At first, I didn't know what he was saying, but I soon figured out I was missing the last part of the word because he was barely breathing it. Down! Jesus, he was saying "Down!"

"See, me and my little brother used to play this game all the damn time, boys," Mack said, his voice loud. I was thankful for his volume. I could follow it. Follow it really well. "We passed down our love for this game to my nephews. Strange how the retarded one was better at it than Ryan."

I was on my belly, slithering my way under the Honda when I started to understand what Mack was saying.

"You put my li'l brother in the hospital, you fucking waste of life!" Mack roared. The flashlight snapped on. I had just curled my legs up as the beam played over where they had been. I tried to contain my breath as I pulled myself out on the other side of the car.

I could feel Eddy leave my side, whispering, "Tire," as he did. I slid down the car with my back against the doors, until I felt the wheel well behind me.

Mack turned his light off again and laughed. "Damn, you boys are good at this!" The soles of his shoes made a shushing noise as he slid across the pavement. "My dad never could keep his dick in his pants. Pardon my French, o' course. The old man would fuck anything that moved. Jude's momma included. I don't ever think that old Mrs. Lance told her husband about my pa. Nah, she kept that hush hush. But Pa told Jude and me about it. Now, where are you?"

The flashlight beam flooded the area under the car. I saw Eddy draw his knees to his chest, keeping his legs close together as he hid behind the tire. I did the same, sucking in my gut to make myself smaller. The sudden rush of wind made me dizzy.

"Damn, you boys should make a fucking sport of this shit!" Mack turned off the light.

The wind shifted as Eddy brushed by me, grabbing my arm as he passed. Pulling me around to the back of the car, he pushed me up and into the trunk with all his force.

Right into Emily Harper's remains.

I caught the bile rising in the back of my throat as my hands splayed out in front of me, sliding in something far too sticky and foul for my liking. I was shoved to the side as Eddy climbed in next to me. I heard a barely audible squeak of metal and felt my breath bouncing back at me off of something that wasn't there before.

Eddy had pulled down the trunk. We were stuck in there with a dead woman and a madman walking around outside.

"I'm the reason little brother went into the National Guard instead of the Army. He seen my pretty face and just knew the Guard was the way to go. Some thought he did it for that bitch of a wife of his. But nah, he did it so he wouldn't have to piece himself back together like they had to do with my face. Then, he got sent to war, anyway. It took me blowing that cunt's head off to get him home!"

Things were getting worse. Mack was letting out too much information. There was no way he was going to let us live. Whatever semblance of hope that remained for our survival disappeared with every nasty little detail he related.

"She was going to turn him in. I had no other choice, really. See, she went and found those goddamn pictures of the boys, same ones you found, Trey, I'm sure of that. She came in to talk to me—me, of all people—and I knew just what to do. Sure, baby brother liked the younger ones, but what was I gonna do, right? He's family, for Christ's sake! Gotcha!"

Light filtered in through the small crack in the trunk space. Distantly, I worried that Mack would realize the trunk wasn't open anymore, but when the light died again, I settled down a little. A soft click came from beside me, and somehow I knew it was Eddy cocking the hammer of the revolver.

"Hooey, you fuckers—pardon my French, o' course—but, you two, boy, you... are... good! Only real effin' champs can hide in a room with only a damn car in it. What am I gonna do with you two? Gotta find you, I s'pose. That's the first order of business!"

"He's coming," Eddy whispered into my ear. Something squished under me, and I gagged. Eddy clapped a hand over my mouth. "Shh…"

The *clop, clop, clop* of Mack's shoes stopped just outside of the trunk. He was playing games with us. The asshole knew exactly where we were.

"Think I didn't notice the trunk was closed, boys?" he whispered through the crack. The smell of cherry lozenges flooded the small compartment.

"Turn it on," Eddy grunted. "The fucking flashlight. Gimme some light."

I flicked on the flashlight, and the small compartment exploded with light. The trunk flew up as Eddy drove his back into it. He rose like a phoenix from the ashes, firing shot after shot.

Mack didn't stand a chance. His shirt exploded as the bullets tore into him.

I didn't think Eddy knew how to use a handgun, but it didn't really matter at that range. He just had to point and pull. He did just that. I blinked against the muzzle flashes as fire licked from the end of the revolver. Six shots total came before they were followed up with the metallic click of the hammer on spent chambers.

Eddy screamed, wailing like a damaged man, even as the gun continued to *click, click, click*.

"Eddy," I moaned, my ears ringing, the *clicks* sounding more like *thumps* as my hearing came and went. I placed a shaky hand on his forearm and pulled. "Eddy. Stop."

Eddy crawled out of the trunk and went to Mack's side. In the flashlight's glow, Mack Larson lay still. The ragged front of his shirt looked as though he'd gotten into the losing end of a fight with a rabid dog. The light bounced up and down as I pulled myself out of the mess that was the Harper girl. When I straightened again, I found Eddy kneeling beside Mack, pulling the gun from the man's still fingers.

Mack had caught a round in the throat, four in the chest, and one had gone through his Nam scar and exited out the back of his head. He was almost certainly dead, but Eddy put two more rounds in the guy's forehead with the gun he had taken.

"My name's Eddy Treemont, motherfucker. Remember that shit on your way to hell." Eddy spit on the dead cop's face, then turned to me, flashing those wonderfully beautiful bucked-teeth.

Chapter Seventeen: Hope

Eddy and I both seemed to remember Jenna at the same time. Our eyes met, and we made a silent connection. We ran over and dropped down beside her, hoping for just one more miracle, one shining beacon in a world gone black.

"Jen?" Eddy put Mack's gun in the waistband of his jeans, flush with his back. He pulled Jenna's head into the palm of his hand.

She coughed, spraying his shirt with blood. "Murphy," she huffed. "I'm all fucked up."

"Huh?" I asked, shaking my head in confusion.

"What?" She actually grinned. "Your folks never let you watch *Robocop*? Not the best movie for kids, I s'pose."

"Damnit, woman, you had us shittin' our pants!" Eddy yelled, but I could see the relief in his face. I was sure he could see it in mine, too.

"Not quite... outta the woods yet, kiddo." Jenna choked up another mass of blood and spit between her legs as she sat up with Eddy's help. "He fucking dead?"

"As hell," Eddy assured her.

"Good." She smiled, blood looking bright on her pale face. "Never did like that asshole, truth be told."

"How we getting out of here?" I asked, coming back to the urgency of the situation.

"We have a perfectly good car sitting there. Long as the battery is still good," Eddy responded.

"The key's... in it?" Jenna groaned.

"Hang on." I went to check. Hanging from the ignition was a set of keys with a pink rabbit's foot dangling from the chain. "Score!"

Then I noticed the gearshift and remembered the clutch I'd seen earlier. "Either one of you know how to drive a stick?"

"Ah, fuck." Jenna coughed.

"Dad's Ford is a manual. He taught me how to work it since Mom couldn't get the hang of it. You know, in case shit happened to him. So we're good." That was Eddy, Mr. Good News all over again.

"You're a... damn life saver, kiddo," Jenna said between ragged breaths. "Help a girl up?"

Eddy and I dipped our heads under her shoulders and ushered her to the open driver's side door. I pulled the seat forward and slid in while Eddy managed Jenna. Once I was settled, I helped pull her in on top of me, while Eddy held her legs. It was tight, but we fit.

"Never thought you'd be laying in my lap by the end of this night." I grinned down at her as she rested her head on my thighs.

"Don't push your luck, Trey." She coughed. "Not nice to take advantage of a... dying girl."

"Ah, you ain't dying. Not for real."

"Tell that to the skeleton in the hoodie standing at my feet. Wonder if he plans on shaving with that blade of his." She laughed, spitting up more blood as she did.

"Grim reaper humor. Nice. See? You ain't so bad after all."

"Tell that to my gut, Trey."

Eddy stepped into the car and slammed the door behind him while I kept talking to Jenna. The Civic struggled, but after a turn or two, it rumbled to life. Eddy ground the first gear, found the right one, and the car finally lurched forward.

We got about two feet before it died, shuddering.

"Sorry," Eddy said. "I let off the clutch too soon."

"Thought you... knew how to drive this thing," Jenna chided.

"You still alive back there? Really?" Eddy grinned at us in the rear view before restarting the car. "Let's try this again."

We jumped forward, and by the grace of God, we kept going. Eddy flipped on the headlights, and the chamber filled with blinding light. Turning sharp to the right, Eddy headed the way Mack had come in for his ambush. Eddy was on the right track. Mack had gotten down there somehow.

The thought of the first tunnel played through my mind, how it had narrowed before opening up again into the chamber. So far, the one Eddy turned the car into didn't look like that. We started climbing, the grade becoming steeper and steeper, until I finally saw cloudy sky ahead in the distance.

And then Mack's cruiser blocked our way.

The thing was parked across the opening, engine running and lights blazing. Thick exhaust plumed from the rear, looking like dragon's breath.

The thought occurred to me almost instantly. Normally, I had to wait around for a good idea, but not that time. "Lemme out," I told Eddy.

"What?" Eddy asked.

"The cruiser." I pointed through the windshield. "It has a radio. I can call for help. The local fire department will get here faster than we can get Jenna to the hospital. They have the shit to help her until they get her to Harmony."

"Sounds... like a plan." Jenna coughed.

Eddy let the engine die and pulled up on the parking brake. The car leaned back a little, and I was worried the brake didn't work, but it held. Eddy came around to the passenger side and pulled the seat forward. Jenna was able to sit up as I slid out, using the doorframe as leverage.

I saw a glimmer of hope as I walked over to the cruiser. I firmly believed Jenna was going to be all right. I believed it was all over. Mack was dead. The good guys had won. The end.

I pulled open the squad car door and yanked the CB from its holder. I hoped it was on the right channel.

"Anybody out there?" was all I could think to say. I sounded like the singer from Pink Floyd.

"I read you. Who is this? Over," a man's voice squawked.

"Need fire and ambulance out at the Westerns." Then, another great idea came to mind. "Officer down!"

Chapter Eighteen: The End

We were going to be heroes; I was certain. How could we not be? It was in the cards. A fact. Done deal.

The Westerns lit up like Christmas in July. The passageway Mack had used let out just on the other side of Juniper. I left Eddy with Jenna as I rounded the bend and met up with the EMTs and responding officers back at the Explorer. They let me ride in the fire truck, and I gave them directions to where Jenna was.

Explaining the long, drawn-out, convoluted story was no fun, but once they got their eyes on Emily Harper, her car, and Officer Mack's remains, the rest was, as they say, history.

They were wheeling Mack Larson away when Hap Carringer pulled up in his brown cruiser. His gray hair was tussled about his head, his Red Sox cap gone, leaving behind a red ring across his wrinkled forehead. His eyes were bloodshot.

When he got a good look at Mack's body under the white sheet, Old Hap lost his shit. Not one of his better moments. He cried. Oh, how he cried.

Then, he wanted answers. We told him everything. All of it. From beginning to end. We didn't miss a beat. Toward the end, Hap looked pretty bad, but he seemed to be coping.

"You boys are gonna have to give statements," Hap finally said, his aged voice cracking with pent-up emotion. "I s'pose I can give you a ride to the station."

I felt sorry for the old man. He'd trusted Mack with everything, had even handed over the key to the city, given the man his vote of confidence. And Mack Larson had repaid him by being a dirty cop. I didn't think I could hate that vile bastard any more, but seeing Hap that way just angered me further.

We followed Hap to his cruiser. The old guy even opened the rear door for us. Eddy slid in first, and I followed. Hap slammed the door behind us. I watched through the iron guard that separated us from the front seats as Hap got in, his old bones popping.

It wasn't until we were on Main Street again that I realized something was wrong. I watched in confusion as every street that could possibly lead to our houses flew by. Hap continued to pick up speed as he drove north, heading out of town.

"Hap?" I spoke up from the back seat. "You missed our turn."

"Really?" Hap grinned at me in the rearview mirror. Something was wrong in his face, in his eyes. Something I'd never seen in him. "Well, don't that just fucking beat all. Pardon my French, o' course."

My blood turned to ice in my veins. I couldn't think straight. Something didn't add up. Hap was singing a song I didn't know the lyrics to. I felt out of place, odd in the stomach, and I knew that very moment that things had gone terribly wrong.

"Oopsy. Did I ruin the big surprise?" Hap glared at me from the rearview mirror. "Never could hold water. Or keep my dick in my pants, for that matter."

"Oh, no fucking way!" Eddy slumped back in his seat, defeated.

"My boys weren't the best of the goddamn lot, but they didn't deserve getting disfigured and killed over it."

I shook my head. "I knew Mack Larson's parents. They were teachers."

"Summer, many a year ago, I got caught in the haystack with Mrs. Larson while the hubby was away. She was a nice piece of ass. Married ones always are. Safer that way, lest the husband finds out." Hap laughed, but it soon turned into a coughing fit. I silently prayed he'd just have a heart attack right then and there. Though he may run us up a tree in the process, I didn't care. At least we'd be free from the crazy bastard.

"Best piece I had was Jude's momma, though. God, she could use them lips. But I'm sure you boys don't know nothing about that, do you?"

We both remained silent. It was our right, after all.

"Jude turned out to be less than I'd hoped for," Hap reminisced. "Always was fond of the young'uns. See, I knew he was fucking round with that Waters girl, so I had to keep tabs on her. When I seen you three running through Rifle Park, trying to beat the goddamn devil, I knew you was up to no good. Low and behold, I find Mack all fucked up, his car seat blown to shit and

366

some dead girl in a blue car, her head all this way and that. Law's mercy, that was a mess. Mack went and had one of them Nam flashbacks when he heard those cherry bombs you kids set off. He just reacted like he was trained. You hear gunfire. You shoot back."

"You got a fucked up family tree," Eddy said, leaning forward.

"Fuck you!" Hap bellowed. "You killed my one good boy, you little shit." Hap yanked the car off of Main Street and onto a dirt road to the left. He was headed to Hunter's Point.

"I cleaned it up like I'm s'pose to do, being a good pa and all. Thought I was done with the matter. But no! You lot gotta come stirring the bottom of the kettle when the soup's been burnt!" The cruiser rocked up and down, side to side, as he raced up the incline.

"Now, I got no other choice but to clean up this mess, too! Everything's gonna come out now. All it takes is a little digging, you little sumbitches. Nobody's done it so far 'cause no one had a fucking reason to!"

Eddy saw what was coming before I did. He twisted in his seat, pulled Mack's gun from his waistband, and aimed it at the back of the Hap's head. "Stop the fucking car, asshole."

"Or what?" Hap cackled. The sound made gooseflesh creep up my arm. "You'll shoot ol' Hap? Go ahead, boy, 'cause this ride don't stop for nobody!"

Hap tramped the accelerator.

Coming to my senses, I grabbed Eddy's arm. "Don't, man. You kill him, *we* die." If he shot Hap, the car would continue whether the old man was in this world or not.

Eddy looked at me, realization pouring over his face, and I watched helplessly as he pointed the gun at my head.

"Pa's gonna make everything right! Pa's got everything pretty fucking covered!" Hap squealed.

The old Crown Vic roared up the dirt road, spraying mud as it went.

"Dammit, Trey, duck!" Eddy yanked me toward the floorboards.

I don't know why I didn't argue with him. It was one of those Eddy-knows-best moments, and I just had to trust the little shit.

The gunfire was deafening. Glass exploded, raining over me. Eddy had shot out my window.

"Go on. Hurry up." Eddy pushed me toward the door.

"You want me to jump?"

"It's that or go off the edge. Fucking go! Whataya looking at, shithead?"

"I'm coming home, Mack," Hap Carringer squealed from the front seat. "Make room for yer pa!"

I drew my knees up under me and twisted toward my salvation. The door caught me in the gut as I dove forward. I hung halfway out the window, watching Hunter's Point coming up quick.

We weren't going to make it.

The cruiser hit a deep hole, and I was ejected from the window.

I hit the ground spinning, rolling like a tumbleweed. The stitches on the back of my neck opened. My right arm bent at a horrible angle, and my shoulder dislocated. I was a screaming, rolling disaster.

Through all the pain, all the anger, all the fear, came thoughts of Eddy. I struggled to push myself off the ground with my one good arm, blood pouring down the back of my neck in torrents. I straightened and faced the direction the car had gone just in time to see the taillights drop out of sight as Hap Carringer's brown cruiser took that crazy old man to his grave.

And Eddy right along with him.

Epilogue

I could go in strenuous detail about how Eddy died, but the facts are simple. Hunter's Point led to a two-hundred-foot drop into nothingness. No one could have survived. Not even Eddy. I don't care how tough that kid was.

I could tell you how I reacted, but it's a moot point. I'd just watched my best friend die, taken from me by the patriarch of a psychotic family that had wrecked everything good in my entire life. You do the math.

I could tell you that I stumbled down to the dirt road and collapsed on the side of the highway until Bay's End's finest showed up to find out what the big bang was all about. That big bang? Oh, that was just Eddy. He always knew how to leave an impression.

They buried Eddy that Saturday. It was a simple gathering. Sanders showed with his parents. I went with Mom and Dad. Eddy's mom cried while his dad sat very quiet, and very drunk, alongside his boy's casket. Do you really blame him?

Jenna wanted to come, but she'd lost a kidney when Mack shot her in the gut. Though you could still survive just fine with only one filter, they wouldn't let her go. She didn't miss much. Besides, she barely knew him.

Everything came out. Everything.

They buried Hap and Mack the Wednesday after they lowered my best friend into the ground. The End didn't know how to cope with the loss of two pillars of the community, both of whom had ended up being part of one big messed-up family. The story was in all the papers from Bay's End to Chestnut, and we were the talk of the county for a good two weeks. Then, as people always do, they moved on.

Sanders's father moved them out of Bay's End and into a condo out in California. We wrote back and forth for a while, but that ended, too, after only two months.

I was alone. No Candy. No Eddy. Nothing but tarnished memories and a haunted brain.

My shoulder healed up fine, along with my neck and leg. It took another twenty-five stitches to close my neck again, but hey, what are you going to do? Now every time it rains, the back of my neck itches, and my shoulder throbs. The shit you take with you, huh? The area on my leg has been numb since they took out the catgut. I still rub the scar from time to time hoping I'll feel something. Anything.

Jude Lance is actually up for parole this year. I have the date circled in red marker on the calendar in my kitchen. I wouldn't miss that party for the fucking world.

I just happened to look back, and the bed is empty. Eddy's ghost is gone. He didn't even say goodbye. What an asshole, huh?

And that, as they say, is that. For all intents and purposes, my final story. It's been real, and it's been fun, but hasn't been real fun. Love it or hate it; it is what it is. And all that shit.

So, in tribute to that beautiful kid with buck teeth and wire rims, I salute you with a middle finger and leave you with this final question.

"Whataya looking at, shithead?"

CPSIA information can be obtained
at www.ICGtesting.com
Printed in the USA
BVHW030214260121
598763BV00010B/45